ASAROTICA

ASAROTICA

EDITED BY ASA AKIRA

Published in the United States by Cleis Press, an imprint of Start Midnight, LLC, 101 Hudson Street, Thirty-Seventh Floor, Suite 3705, Jersey City, NJ 07302.

Printed in the United States.
Cover design: Scott Idleman/Blink
Cover photograph: iStock
Text design: Frank Wiedemann
First Edition.
10 9 8 7 6 5 4 3 2 1

Trade paper ISBN: 978-1-62778-226-5
E-book ISBN: 978-1-62778-227-2

Library of Congress Cataloging-in-Publication Data is available on file.

TABLE OF CONTENTS

FOREWORD

"What turns women on?"

"What do men masturbate to?"

"What do porn stars think about in their most intimate moments?"

It's a silly idea, assigning sexual fantasies exclusively to specific groups of people. But when your profession is sex, you get these questions often.

As a cis-woman in porn falling somewhere on the scale between straight and bisexual, I have erotic thoughts that might be considered outrageous to some and boring to others. I don't see desire as limited to gender, class, or even sexual orientation. It's not as simple as saying, "Women find submission hot," or "Only men like feet." People are all unique, from various backgrounds with differing inclinations and motivators. As individuals we enjoy different flavors of food, listen to different genres of music, clothe ourselves in different types of outfits. Why would all of our sexual fantasies be the same?

So, you ask, what do porn stars find erotic? In these

twenty-two short stories I've curated, you'll find the simple answer to a complex question: Everything. The stories in this collection are anything but your typical erotic fiction, and I'm proud of that. They're original, authentic, and often challenge our ideas of what we perceive as "normal," and sometimes even "ethical"—which I find beautiful. Erotic writing is a fun, safe, sexy outlet for us to play out our most unconventional fantasies, and in editing this book, I censored exactly none of them.

I hope you enjoy.

Asa

THE CENTER

BY ASA AKIRA

He woke up before her, as he always did on Tuesdays. Thirty-two cracks in the ceiling, same as last Tuesday, same as the Tuesday before that, and the Tuesday before that. In her bed, Hana moaned in her sleep and kicked her leg out from under the blanket. She would be awake soon.

She looked so peaceful at this hour, her grey hair pinned up, head on her pillow, face smooth and expressionless. Not like the rest of the day, with that wrinkle in between her eyebrows, which grew even deeper with each year. Never would she say it out loud—not just to Matsu, but to anyone—but he sensed she couldn't remember the last time she was truly happy. That wrinkle, though, she could not hide.

It was an arranged marriage. Thirty-plus years ago, he wondered if she would have agreed to commit to him had she known what the future held in store for them. Probably not.

He had grown to love her. Even before any of it had happened. When she bore his first child, how could he not? She gave him the gift of family. And when that child died of pneumonia, they had grieved together. Some couples were torn apart by such an event, finding themselves unable to move forward together. Not Hana and Matsu.

For certain, by the births of their second and third children, a boy and a girl, he loved her.

"Are you awake?" Hana asked through a yawn.

He closed his eyes and pretended to open them for the first time that morning. He silently counted to three, and groaned.

"Shall we get up?" She stretched.

Matsu groaned again.

Breakfast was the same every day. Coffee with milk. Three slices of white toast—one with Nutella, one with butter, one with jam. On occasion, they had marmalade made by Hana's friend from across the street. Neither of them was particularly fond of citrus-based jams, but they indulged it for the sake of neighborhood politics. Luckily, on this morning, there was no marmalade.

"The van will come half an hour late today," Hana said over her newspaper.

Putting down his own paper, Matsu studied her across the table. The sun was beaming through the window, the birds were chirping. He thought about how her sleeveless shirt did not flatter her old, flabby arms.

"There's an event at the Center today, so pick-up will be late."

Thirty minutes. Thirty extra minutes, he would have to wait.

"Ken is driving up tonight, so you have the grandkids to look forward to as well. They'll be staying with us until Friday."

Ken's kids were all right. Rather, the girl was. The boy, he could do without. Matsu had a feeling right away; as a newborn, the boy hadn't taken to his mother's milk from her breast the way the girl had, almost instantaneously. Two years ago, when she was eight, she asked her grandfather about the abacus sitting at the edge of his desk. After Matsu taught her to use it, she took the abacus and sat at his desk all day, incessantly asking him for more equations. She sat there until he retired to bed. The next day, the abacus was back on the edge of the desk, forgotten.

But she was a child, after all.

The drive to the Center was usually no more than five minutes, but today, because there were two more pickups after Matsu, the trip was over thirty minutes long.

First stop was Jiro. Matsu didn't know much about him, except that he hardly ever spoke at all. I suppose neither do I, he thought as the two locked eyes when Jiro entered the van. The two continued the ride in silence. Outside the window, Matsu noticed a woman walking—her white shirt had partially turned transparent from sweat. He could see her bra was mint green.

Next stop was Kai, who broke the dead air in which Jiro and Matsu had been riding.

"My grandson won first place in a summer camp swimming competition this weekend!" he boasted.

Matsu half smiled, though he didn't care. Not to say he was bitter; he just had no interest in other people's families. He had always been that way.

Before his accident, Kai had been an artist. Losing the use of his hands, he now painted with a brush in his mouth, holding it between his teeth. The paintings weren't bad considering they were painted without hands.

At 12:45, they were the last group to arrive at the Center. Everyone was in the cafeteria already, bibs around their necks, enjoying today's snack: strawberry yogurt. Out of ten total paraplegics, five were being spoon-fed. The other five struggled, with yogurt and drool pouring down their faces and bibs. A band of young girls played instruments and sang a familiar children's song, as some of the Center employees sang along, clapping their hands to the beat.

Sachi came to greet Matsu at the entrance. For the first time in a week, he genuinely smiled from his heart. She wore her usual Center uniform, a tight, crisp white dress that buttoned up the middle. Her stockings and shoes were also white. She wheeled him to a table in the cafeteria, and he wondered if she would pick him again this week. She had the last two, but three in a row? Was that even within the policies of the Center?

Wrapping the paper bib around his neck, Sachi asked him if he'd be good to feed himself today. After he nodded, she walked away. He wondered if he should have said no.

Like the majority of the world, he had been born right-handed. Well, nowadays, they said all children were born ambidextrous—but for as long as he could remember, he had been more comfortable using the right hand. So when the stroke left the entire right side of his body paralyzed nine years ago, Matsu had to relearn everything with the left hand. Writing. Eating. Wiping his ass.

Even now, feeding himself was not a graceful action. Scooping the yogurt onto the spoon, bringing it through the air up to his face, and then delivering it to his mouth—it was still a cumbersome task, nine years later. Only half of his mouth had the power to open, chew, and swallow.

Before he could finish his yogurt, they started to call out names.

Rina was first. "Shin-san, he will take you today." Matsu was relieved. Rina was one of the first he had experienced. Her breath smelled like cigarettes, and her tits were too small. Not that the size of tits affected him in any way. But if her breath was going to stink, her tits could have been at least a C-cup.

As Rina wheeled Shin out of the cafeteria, a few more of the employees called out names and went to greet their paraplegics. Finally, it was Sachi's turn. She walked toward Matsu, bent down, and put her hand on his thigh. He couldn't feel it, for the lower half of his body ceased to have any feeling, but the gesture made him happy.

"May I take you again this week?" she asked.

"Yes please," he meant to respond, but what came out was, "Yegh pee." She understood.

Sachi brought him into a room different from the last time. It was similar in layout, and decorated the exact same way, but he knew this wasn't the same room. Last week, they had taken an elevator. This week, they did not. And this room was colder.

After engaging the brake on his wheelchair in the center of the room, Sachi went to get the vial from the refrigerator.

"Just ten minutes away now," she smiled.

Piercing the top of the vial with the needle, Sachi prepared the shot. Matsu looked around the room, for this part made him nervous. Why this was, he couldn't say—it wasn't like he could feel anything. Not even a phantom pain, which was something some of the others claimed to feel.

"Don't worry," Sachi said. "I'll be gentle." She knew he was incapable of feeling anything, but it was her habit to offer words of comfort. Matsu appreciated it.

Once the needle was full, she placed it on a metallic tray and brought it over to him. After placing the tray on the table, she reached toward his waist and carefully started to lift his shirt.

Matsu stopped her. He meant to say, "I'm a bit cold," but what came out was, "Ahmaa bee coww."

She understood.

"No problem," she said, and untied the string of his pants instead. "Shall we just take your dick out instead of pulling the pants off all the way?"

He meant to answer, "I'd like that," but what came out was, "Agh lagh daagh."

She understood.

Sachi pulled the limp penis out of Matsu's pants. He had stopped wearing underwear once he lost the ability to dress and undress himself—it was just an extra step for Hana every time he needed to use the bathroom.

Looking straight forward as Sachi held a piece of him in her hands, Matsu thought about his dick. Having caught a glimpse here and there of it in the mirror when Hana bathed him, he knew it was pathetic-looking. He was almost sure it never looked this small before the stroke, as if it had never been quite this relaxed before, this flaccid. Sachi reached over to the table, grabbed the needle from the tray, and inserted it into the base of the cock.

Matsu continued to look straight ahead. Not that he had much of a choice. He didn't feel a thing, but hearing Sachi's breathing started to turn him on.

After injecting him, Sachi put the needle down and stepped back. It would be another few minutes before the shot took effect. Looking at him, she slowly unbuttoned her dress. As the buttons opened, more of her white bra was exposed. Sachi's breasts were full and youthful. Unlike Hana's, which, after breastfeeding three children, looked like two empty two grocery bags made of skin.

As Sachi stripped down to nothing, naked, bare, she told him why she had picked him again.

"Some of these guys that come here, they're too into it," she explained. "They're too eager for my taste. I like how you just sit there in silence."

The truth was, Matsu had always been like this, even before he was paralyzed. He had never been much of a talker, or even a moaner. He didn't believe men should make much, if any, noise during sexual activities. It was emasculating.

She sat on top of him, facing away from his face. By her moan he could tell his dick was now hard. She bounced up and down, grinded back and forth. As her breath stopped and her voice squealed as she came, he remembered why he enjoyed this.

He felt like a man again. His heart started to beat faster.

In the metallic tray on the table, he could see a tiny reflection of himself. Sachi riding up and down on his hard cock. Shiny from her pussy juices.

He meant to say, "Turn around," but what came out was, "Taagghhuudd." She understood.

Sachi got up, spun around to face him, and sat down on him again.

He watched her tits bounce in a circular motion, going in opposite ways as she rode him. Looking in the tray again, he could see her asshole. And as she came again, her ass clenched, creating a hundred little dimples in her tight cheeks.

As she came down from orgasming, Sachi grabbed the back of Matsu's neck, threw her legs up over his shoulders, and pushed her pelvis back and forth on him as she whispered in his left ear. "You like the way I fuck you, you fucking gimp?"

Her breath sent a tickle from his ear, all the way down the left side of his body to his waist.

"Tell me I can use your wheelchair cock whenever I want," she whispered.

He meant to say, "My cock is here for your use," but what came out was, "Maa caaghh ii heee foohh goorghhh yuuu." She understood. And continued to grind until she came.

Over the next fifteen minutes or so, he sat there in silence as she violently slammed him into her, enjoying each time his cock gave her another orgasm. When she turned back around to face away from him, he saw beads of sweat trickling down her back. He thought of the woman from earlier with the mint green bra.

Finally she climbed off, tied his pants back on, dressed herself, and wheeled him back into the cafeteria.

A couple of people were already there, waiting to be taken home. It would be another hour or so before their erections went down. Once all the men were gathered in the cafeteria, the young girls started to play children's songs again. The employees, and some of the men, sang along.

One by one, the employees came around to check the dicks, waiting for them to return to their flaccid state. When they were, they were wheeled to the front of the building, where vans drove them home in groups of threes.

PUSSY WITH EXTRA CHEESE, PLEASE

BY JOANNA ANGEL

As Aaron enjoyed his undercover hand job by the stage, he turned toward Aiden to kiss her. He felt that was the polite thing to do when someone was stroking his cock, but Aiden pushed his head back in the other direction and implored, "Don't look at me, just look at Joanna on stage."

She then snuck her other hand underneath her short red dress and into her panties, touching herself while continuing to stroke Aaron's cock.

In this moment I felt like I could be crowned the queen of sex. My ego, my pussy, and my heart were all being stroked in wonderful ways. My sexual energy radiated through the neon blue and green lights of the strip club. I'd traveled all over the world in my lifetime: everywhere from the depths of the Dead Sea in Israel, to the top of the Arc De Triomphe in Paris. But never had I found myself so aroused as I was at that strip club in Tampa, Florida.

Let me back up a second and explain.

When someone in porn enters a relationship with someone

not in porn (a "civilian" is what we call them), there's a unique set of complications that come along with it. It's disturbing if said civilian partner gets off on it, yet it's unbearable if they can't stand it. They basically need to come to the conclusion on their own that cleaning their asshole out with various shower hose attachments before heading to an undetermined mansion with a pool somewhere in Los Angeles to have anal sex with an acquaintance of mine is neither arousing nor unsettling; it's just another day.

This, in itself, is a feat which requires a whole other chapter for another day. But when things got serious with my non-porno boyfriend, we communicated and worked towards making our abnormal situation, well, normal. We cooked dinners at night and shared a dog. He was respectful to the other men I worked with (a.k.a. the professional way of saying, the guys I fuck), and he truly loved and encouraged me unconditionally. You could certainly say I was having my cake and eating it, too.

But I was a horny lady in my dirty thirties. And I still wanted more cake.

Or actually, not cake. I never really had much of a sweet tooth. I wanted cheese.

"So, I am basically, like, 60 percent lesbian," I admitted to Aaron one night as he slaved away in the kitchen cooking me some post-gangbang tacos.

"Really?" he replied as he calmly chopped onions and cilantro.

"Yes, I am. It's complicated. I don't want to date women, but I am more attracted to them than I am to men, and if I go too long without having sex with one I get really cranky."

Aaron continued to chop, and I started to worry I had said too much. Was I being selfish? I had always told him that I really wanted a normal life outside of porn. Just that, my version of a normal life included porn, stripping, having a boyfriend, in addition to the occasional vagina. I mean, that was totally normal, right?

To my surprise, Aaron was incredibly turned on by it. The thing was, because my previous boyfriend—despite being a porn star himself—considered any kind of interaction with anyone off-camera (including iMessaging) cheating, my expectations of men and their egomaniacal needs were pretty low.

God, I really just sounded like a lesbian there.

Upon the realization that my boyfriend was just the perfect level of freak for me, I wanted to find the perfect female for us to share. Most people wouldn't believe me if I told them, but I had a hard time finding women to have sex with. Really, I did!

You see, I'd reached this status in the porn industry where people seemed to really respect me. And while respect is nice . . . sex is better.

I was a director. Directors typically weren't supposed to hit on the talent—it was generally considered bad porn etiquette. If a male director randomly texted a girl who was talent and asked her to come over and fuck, well, that was considered creepy. That was the kind of thing that made girls quit porn, then appear in a documentary one day crying about it. Or maybe they would go through with it and say, "Well I thought I had to, because he was the director."

The negative stigma around all us big bad producers and directors made me quite awkward and hesitant to admit to a girl that I want to throw her against the wall and eat her pussy without any cameras around. It figured—despite being in porn, I could probably get away with being more sexually inappropriate as a general manager at Applebee's.

"Well, you fuck girls all the time on camera," one might argue, but one would be wrong. In fact, I performed very few lesbian scenes because I developed a large following of people who loved seeing me with multiple cocks in and around my face. As a producer of my own content, I had to be very strategic with what kind of sex I should spend my money on, and every time I did choose to spend money on a vagina in my face, it tended to be a loss. People generally related "girl with lots of tattoos" with "girl who should have at least two cocks inside her at all times." And that was all great—I was a fan of two cocks, three cocks, even four cocks, but I truly did love vagina.

I needed it every once in a while.

Being a porn star at the age of thirty-five, I adhered to a strict diet to keep my body camera-appropriate. But once a week, I treated myself to several slices of expensive artisanal cheese. It stopped me from going insane. I felt the same way about vagina.

I was asked to attend a particular adult convention that was taking place at a bunch of strip clubs. Most porn conventions are just like regular conventions. They take place in giant expo halls filled with vendors' booths selling their products—only instead of the products being, like, hot tubs, dental equipment, and comic books, it's porn companies and porn stars selling their movies, autographs, and photos. Like flea markets, but with more tits.

This particular "convention" was different. The company that ran this event did advertising campaigns for strip clubs, so the entire event was held at different gentlemen's clubs throughout Tampa, Florida. Basically, I was more or less told that my "job" for the weekend was to hang out at strip clubs and get drunk.

Producing and directing and performing and running my own company was incredibly time consuming and I had to be selective about the events I chose to attend. Plus, I had a boyfriend that I actually liked. Even loved, perhaps. I tried to spend the little amount of free time that I had with him. And this was an unpaid gig with minimal exposure that would require me to stay up way past my bedtime. But when I was told that my assigned roommate for the trip would be Aiden, there was no question. If vaginas were my cheese, then Aiden's pussy was like a Triple Créme Brie that you could only get from a local market in the countryside of France.

I had met Aiden on a couple of occasions, as both a fellow porn performer and regular person. Her relationship status was always rather complicated because she had a girlfriend, and two boyfriends, and all of these relationships were incredibly intense and— how do I put this?—oddly monogamous. At least two of her three partners fucked only her, and the third was still somehow seriously committed. But though she was most definitely dating all of them, her dance card was clearly full, so I did what any other creepy porn director would do in my situation: I booked her to perform a gratuitous sex scene, with me. So technically, we had sex once. But it was on camera. It counts, but . . . it doesn't count. I'm not quite sure how else to explain it. I was greedy and wanted more and I was about 99.9999999 percent certain that she did too.

Now, my boyfriend jerked off to the scene numerous times. He loved it. Every time I would leave town—or the house for a few hours—the scene was always queued up on his computer. He told me he loved the faces and the sounds I made when she ate my pussy, like they were a completely new set of orgasms to which he hadn't been introduced. The chemistry I had with her excited him, and she excited me in general, and exciting him excited me. So to say the least, knowing I could have her all to myself for a full weekend as a roommate would complete this circle of exciting things I had going on here.

The first night Aiden and I were in Tampa, we did our, um, "jobs." We caravanned to a strip club and hung out with about thirty other porn stars. Things remained playful and innocent. Together we drank watered-down vodka drinks, made out, tipped strippers, made out some more, and then posted some pathetically offbeat six-second twerking videos to Vine, the only place you could post instantaneous video to the internet at the time.

It was basically the Stone Age.

When we got back to our shared hotel room, we kissed, but

ultimately, we went to our respective beds, and I drifted off to sleep as she proceeded to call all three of her paramours to say good night.

The next day, beside the pool, she talked to me about her relationship problems. She confessed that she was sick of everyone falling in love with her, and desperately wanted someone to fuck her and not get attached. I told her I could very easily find not one, but two people who could do that quite happily. She giggled with excitement. I texted my boyfriend who was in Los Angeles and told him to find the fastest way to get to Tampa, Florida. Within two hours, he was on a plane.

Meanwhile, Aiden and I returned to the strip club. The kisses between us that evening were longer, heavier, and with more tongue. The more we kissed, the more our hands started wandering down each other's thighs. My boyfriend came to meet us straight from the airport. I barely got through the introductions when he showed up, "Aiden meet my boyfriend, Aaron—" She grabbed his cock immediately while she and I proceeded to sloppily kiss each other like we were attempting to eat each others faces.

Part of my job that evening was to strip on stage for a few songs. As I climbed the pole and whipped my hair around to Pantera, Aiden and Aaron sat by the stage, Aiden giving Aaron a sly under-the-pants and under-the-stage handjob.

So, like I was saying, as Aaron continued to enjoy his undercover handjob by the stage, he turned towards Aiden to kiss her, but Aiden pushed his head back in the other direction. "Don't look at me, just look at Joanna on stage." She then began touching herself while maintaining her stroke. And like I said, I felt I could be crowned queen of sex at that moment.

Aaron wasn't having a bad evening, either, coming straight from the airport to a strip club, where a handjob awaited him on arrival. But he hadn't eaten, so as soon as we got back to the hotel room, as Aiden and I were tearing off each other's already ripped fishnets and microscopic lace dresses, he surreptitiously ordered a pizza doing his best to not distract us.

He quickly hung up and jumped in. Aiden and I took turns sucking his cock and I pushed her head down on it as far as she could possibly go. We giggled and laughed and fought over his cock. We gathered up all the saliva in our bodies and spit it into each other's mouths, onto his dick, and then back into our mouths. Aiden pushed me down and licked my pussy, finding my clit like she came prepared with a map and directions on how to get there. Aaron fucked her from behind and she belted out a strong orgasm while I simultaneously came in her mouth. I wasn't sure if Aaron was having sex with Aiden and me, or if Aaron and I were having sex with Aiden

It's difficult to find a perfect threesome partner when you're in a relationship. Just because I am a porn star it doesn't mean I don't get jealous, and if I start to feel like my relationship is being disrespected, my fluid sexual energy becomes cold and frigid. It's hard to put my finger on exactly when those moments happen but they do. One strange kiss, one off look in someone's eyes, can kill the threesome's Feng Shui. On this occasion, however, it was a beautiful musical of tits and ass and pussy working together in perfect harmony.

Aiden's pussy was fucked to the point where it was just quivering and couldn't accept any more dick. He then plunged his cock inside me. Like always, Aaron's cock fit like a glove. My vagina was all, "Welcome home, cock!" He fucked and fucked, and then . . .

The phone rang.

The pizza had arrived.

"You guys keep doing what you're doing," he said gleefully. "I'll be back!"

Aaron threw on some jeans that barely fit over his boner and ran downstairs. I licked Aiden's pussy and shoved my fingers in and out of her, and all the while, we just couldn't stop kissing. Aaron ran back into the room, threw the pizza box on the floor, ripped his pants off, and jumped back in.

We attempted to resume with the same energy we had before, but we were all moving a little bit slower, the smell of pizza wafting through the air taking precedence over the wafting pussy. We simultaneously came to a stop, everyone thinking the same thing.

"Let's eat some pizza," Aiden said.

After that brief intermission we got back into it. I came several more times, and then, eventually, Aaron finished in both of our mouths—a tasty combination of tomato sauce, mozzarella cheese, and jizz.

Aiden smiled, giggled, and jumped off the bed, reaching again for the pizza box. She grabbed one of the few remaining slices for herself and handed me and Aaron the rest. She scampered off into her own respective bed just a few feet away from ours. We ate the remainder of our pizza, watching episodes of Married with Children as our bodies drifted into a sex-and-carbs-induced slumber.

Aiden left early in the morning and returned home to her trifecta of monogamy. We still hang out every once in awhile when the stars align properly (or improperly, depending on the way you look at it), but our night in Tampa will always be remembered as the night my 60-percent-lesbian was happiest.

GLASS AGAINST NIGHT

BY KAYDEN KROSS

That night brought me back to him. My car eased into his driveway as I pushed my tongue into the cut where the blood had run and hit the chassis on the curb. I thought about the ways blood might have gotten there. One way was me. The rip along the lining of my cheek matched the shape of my teeth.

My car rolled forward, crunching birch leaves blackly in the tracks where the tires tread. I turned the key back. The headlights clicked off first and then the cabin light. Bushes pushed up dark veils beyond the window, and the house was speared against the side of a cliff. The driveway sloped down. I pushed my foot into the parking brake and stared into the black shadowed mass just before me. He was in there, somewhere, maybe a part of it. All of the lights were out but the moon was up, cutting in and out between the clouds. I used the glow to find a footpath.

Past the gravel there were stepping stones and then a system of steps that descended towards a door whose color wasn't clear even in the light that pushed down as the clouds moved or in the gleam at the door where brass glinted in the sweep. I raised my fist. The door felt like the stone front of a tomb. What was his life like behind it? With a small palm I choked my hair at the neck and pushed the weight of it back behind my shoulder, shuddering when it swung at the low place where my skin dipped against my spine. I tucked my chin down and waited, wondering what this man does in these times, alone, left to drop the civilities and the affects and just be a body with small and mundane bodily tasks and small and mundane human thoughts. Was he human in the messy ways? From the hills just beyond, a pack of coyotes sang sharply skyward of its kill. Still further lay mountains jutting black and skyward too, and somewhere just behind them the moon was pulling waves up from the sea. Each was in the midst of some beggar's blind bid toward ascension. You could see it down to the details, in the daytime as salt turned to crystal in the heat waves. You could see it in the ruptures pushing out gas from the mountaintops and in the notes in the throats of each predator sending off mythos and the souls of prey. That was the year I made my bid, too. I raised a fist again. The door pushed in where it hit.

Inside, the air was still. The space was expansive and dark save a faint umber gloss straining outward from the mouth of a room at the end of a hall, the likely spill of one low recessed light in his bedroom ceiling. The light was one set so that all that could be seen of another person was a slight glint in the eyes and the curves and planes of the flesh. The light was his choosing. The rays waned indifferently onto the tile, moving smoothly forward in measured squares. They gave off the telltale deception of a structure stuck in time, of muddled origin, still as a dried river or some past god's great cathedral floor. Where I walked I watched it extend under my feet and past me, spreading gently away from my center in every direction. My feet made no noise. I followed the light through the length of the hall and through his bedroom door. I cast a shadow without an edge.

He stood with his back to me, shirtless, busied with his phone. His hair was black against the moonlight that outlined the bodily way it moved when he did, outlined the lines and bulges of his shoulders, the taper at his waist, the heavy biceps that pulled the device away and pressed it back against his ear between the space where he spoke to me. He nodded dismissively in the direction of another door off the other end of the room. Behind him, the wall facing the mountains was made of glass.

He said, "Get in the shower."

His eyes were black too, though in the light they became a vital brown that sparked beneath the shadow of his brow. His frame was tall, his lips thick. I pushed off my shoes and my clothes and padded barefoot over stone that faded from amber now to a clouded marble in the moonlight. They steamed up faintly around the shape of my foot and dissolved again. The night was cold. I noticed my skin against the air, white too now in the moonlight, and my ankles lifting my feet from their steps. My ankles were thin.

The faucet turned easily. The walls there were the continued length of the glass that faced the mountainside. Another coyote offered its song up from the rocks, and then there were more. They faded out. With spread fingers I checked the temperature as the water ran rivulets along my wrist. Another twist of the hardware and the shower-head streamed. Hot wet drops fell out in ropes. The water made a low-tunneled noise.

His fingers slipping through my hair were the first sign that he was there. They spread out widely and pushed until his palm pressed up flush with my skull. In another moment they snapped back, locking my hair into his grip. He wrapped the length across his fist, and then again, laying it flat and tight across the knuckles. His wrists were deliberate. They exposed my face. Where the shower water hit on tile, it sprayed back up. I was wet at the ankles, wet up the legs, wet with the drops that clung to the hair that rose when I shuddered. He brought me to his mouth. His lips pushed us down beneath the water and his tongue pushed down into my throat. The space was empty of air. When he pulled back I sucked in my breath as he tilted my face towards the window. Slanting moonlight hit thick streams against my skin. He held my chin with a finger, a fist still gripped in my hair, as he guided my face from side to side. He pushed my chin up and the planes were smooth. They turned to blue in the curves. Time slowed as he examined me, tilted me, decided on me, and then the seconds accelerated again and brought us present as his grip tightened and his eyes locked on mine.

One of us blinked. There was the force of sound and heat and of air as he shifted behind me, pressing his skin against my skin, at my throat locked in the crook of his arm so that my head lifted back and pressing at the cartilage in a way that his slightest move was the difference between my breathing and not. I couldn't see him but I felt where he watched me. My hands rested on his arms, the fingers soft. There was no struggle. The air was still cool against the skin. He reached down to his belt and pulled it loose, leather sliding through each hoop with a sound of release and the metal on the buckle clinking thinly against itself. He made no other noise. Then his hand was in my hair again, my body dragged along behind his grip while in the other grip he dragged the belt. I came stumbling into the position he dropped me, eye-level now with the unbuttoned front of his pants, ear pressed against his hip, cool marble at my knees. Water still thrashed in hard streams in the background, and black mountains looked on from a distance through the glass. We faced his bed. With a flick of his wrist I was spun around at the base, his grip knotted in my hair. The belt drifted its dead leather end across my lap as he used the buckle to open my jaw, pressing metal between my lips. I opened. He shifted back and then pushed into me. Repeatedly and forcefully he shoved me throat-first down onto the destructive length that emerged from him, steadfast, the shift throwing me off balance and deeper down, my ass forced up as he doubled the leather and unleashed its whips down the length of me, each blow pushing me forward and pulling up thickly strung spit and each break rocking me back off enough to grasp at air and arch back up for more.

When welts lined my flanks and both cheeks of my ass, he pulled me to the bed by the hair and came down pressing with his wrist against my throat. He held me down hard. I lifted my chin to give him room. His eyes watched mine. On the pullback I was met with a heavy wall of blood rushing on lungs, my chest kicking and heaving for air. I could feel the night. There were the light shafts shifting through the glass and the ridge of the mountainside pushing up. The colors were notes that descended a scale from the lunar pale of the moonlight to the watery blues that deepened down into black. They each had a name. My skin tingled along the tracks where he'd touched. The trails were proof of life. Now he was moving against me hard and fast with his chest flush with mine, sweat sliding between us as his mouth brushed against my ear with the stream of low-pitched words that he spoke. When he'd gone dry of words they faded to whispers, small syllables thrust in time to his movements whose sounds eventually were no longer words but the weight of his own laboring breath as he moved his mouth down the side of my neck and bit into my throat. The skin below him burned with the suction he built into blood darkened marks. He pulled me back gasping, grabbing my gaze with a force that stopped my lungs. He wrapped my neck in his grip. Pushing back, I moved my chin towards the sky to give him room. There we stayed, locked in a single outcome, hung now on the dull slush of blood rushing on lungs, blind fingers searching the blackness for air, screaming with that growing need as my eyes became hot and my veins thick and his eyes too became fevered burning with a hungered pitch.

He inhaled first before he let me breathe. He said a word. When I sucked in, I took the air that came from him.

Every bottomless breath poured in louder than the last. What rushed in with the oxygen would cause me to pull him closer and need it again. There was ascension. There was the high at the edge of death and the last prayer that the soul casts in for the body before it leaps. There was the indiscriminate outline between my shadow and the dark. There was the ether. I pulled his hand back to my throat and he removed it. I pulled again.

Push me.

His eyes narrowed and he pulled back, smacking me sharply across the cheek before he grabbed my face and pushed his fingers in, cradled the angle of my chin into his palm. Dully I tasted the blood flow where my teeth reopened the cut that lined my cheek. I parted my lips and pulled his tongue in too.

With a hand hooked behind my head he brought his forehead to mine. His movement slowed and his eyes stayed even with mine, held mine, pushed through mine with the same deliberations that his body made, the quiet ebb and flow of the flesh pushing into the pull and retreating, coming back again, the steady build of feeling rising to a tipping point, the exhilaration of the cliff's edge, that pinnacle atop descent.

He pulled his head back and spat.

The heat of his mouth ran streams across my cheeks and through my hair. A string hung down from his lips and he let it, his jaw pushed forward, his gaze hard. I stared back. He spat again, then dried his lips against his arm. He cupped a palm on my hip and sunk his fingers in before flipping me over, shoving my face down, wrapping my hair again into his fist as he leaned forward with a forearm strung under my waist. With a sharp jerk he pulled my ass up and my head back at once, shaping me into the form he wanted, creating me before he thrust, and I braced by pushing into him too and gripping the sheets with my teeth.

Where his lips touched my back he bit down and he held, pulling air across my skin when he sucked in. His teeth left individual impressions in rough parentheses, surrounding the spidering of broken veins and the curling lift of broken skin. His skin was hot and he trembled. I arched deeper into him and he pushed in turn, feeling for the heated center between us. He stayed there, teasing the edge of it, dipping in and pulling out without submerging, dangling the promise of it. In another breath he pushed me back.

I curled fetally and begged for him. I needed him most then. I needed him to do worse, and I needed more. He responded to the way my words cracked with the rawness in my throat. Rising up on his knees, he put a hand on his cock and extended the other in my direction, luring me forward while he made small strokes at the head of his cock as if treading, holding himself in some place far above me. My begging came through in a low rocking voice. I set myself in front of him. There he watched me as his hands inched slowly along my back, smoothed over the bites and the welts, the long thin red lines left in the wake of where his fingers had dragged on my hips, holding the heat in, leaning back against the wall that held him in. He stopped. The room darkened with the moon as it passed behind a cloud. Wind kicked up just past the glass, howling through the gullies down below. It sounded like the scream of something caught and then it stilled. Both of us breathed.

The moonlight was moving again when he lifted his hand with a wave of force. He came down heavily, fist forced against the muscle of my ass. His eyes glinted at the feel of that. He raised his fist again and struck, again and again, frenzied, building his force and his speed until without warning he stopped and pulled me up to eye level by the throat.

"Tell me you're mine."

Yes. I said, "Yes yes yes yes yes yes," in a low murmur. I lost the precious last of the air in my lungs with each word as he lowered me back down and dragged me again by the hair back to the water still steaming and spitting in the shower, pushed me under the stream and cleaned my face as he demanded again, "Are you mine? Are you mine? Say it."

"Yes. I'm yours I'm yours I'm yours I'm yours."

The words came broken through the spit strung on my lips. He dropped me down to my knees. My skin scraped on the tile. I opened my mouth to reach him and he shoved me back.

He made me stay.

The floor was cool and it seeped in through my skin. Outside the night air was cooler still. There was just that glass to hold it back. I imagined looking into that blackness every night. I thought of my palm against the glass, the shape of the print it would leave. Was there a finite amount of heat you could take from a body? The clouds shifted again and blocked out the moonlight before they moved on further. Something with talons and wings soared up against the sky but made no noise. The only noise was in that room.

"Mine," he said, his hand gripped thickly on that length. He watched me.

I nodded, face tilted up for him, waiting.

He kept me there as the faint bit of moonlight caught in his eyes. His eyes held mine. With a heavy hand he turned the faucet and the water died. The world was silent now outside of my whispers, pleading, my hands clasped at my elbows behind my back, the world was silent around the edge of my mouth barely moving with the words. I tasted blood. The taste was mixed with his. I could feel the heat coming off his skin. The one thing he couldn't will away was his own dogged heat. He had a hand on his cock.

"What would you do for me?"

"Anything."

"Anything?"

I nodded again.

When he spilled it fell across my face and my scalp, gathering in wet ropes and gaining speed down my chest and back and making pools at my knees, hot wet piss spreading as he said to me, "Mine." I leaned forward and into it, taking everything he would give me, whispering as it gushed in through my lips and my mouth, as it followed the lines of my upturned jaw, whispering with only the movement of the push of air up against the back of my lips and with the strain of my vocal chords trying not to stretch in my throat, whispering, "Please."

When he was done, he held my chin between his thumb and forefinger and moved my face side to side in the moonlight. After a long calm look he pulled me in. Guiding my mouth onto his cock he made a few thick strokes before he came and I swallowed that, too.

THE FAMILY TRIO

BY TASHA REIGN

"Happy Fourth of July, Rachel!" my bestie Annabelle yelled.

It was a perfect day in Malibu (or "The Bu," as my friends and I called it): eighty degrees, the sun shining, dolphins sporadically jumping out of the water. I was twenty-six years old and had finally graduated college. Armed with a Masters in Journalism, my dream job as the editor of a small hipster magazine called *Millennials Now* awaited me, and I celebrated with my friends—more friends than anyone could ask for. I was grateful, blessed, and every high emotion in between. Mostly.

Intellectually, I understood it was 2016, and that a boyfriend wasn't a necessary component to happiness. But I'd grown up with the Disney movie idea of romance and the hope remained that a dreamy prince would one day sweep me off my feet.

Plus, I was a total perv. Every time I met someone, I couldn't help but picture them getting fucked, or giving it to someone in the back of an alley. Despite my sunny California upbringing, I was super attracted to the hardcore, vulgar sexuality of life. I was even a closet porn fan—the medium was a great way to get my fix of the strange and unfamiliar. Only my close friends knew about my . . . hobby.

On that particular, glorious summer day, I was basking in the ambiance of the oceanfront mansion to which I had been invited—designer cocktails, delectable appetizers, and of course, the hottest bachelors in all of Los Angeles county. They were literally tall, dark, handsome . . . and rich.

It was a tradition every year for Annabelle's parents to throw this soiree, and it was my tradition at this annual gala to make an appearance looking my best, and socializing like a true pro. This year, however, I would be looking to score, and at five-foot-seven, with long blonde hair, bright green eyes with a just hint of a blue, and the best boobs ever, I could get any man to notice me, even if I was dressed in a burka. Not to brag or anything, but I was a total smoke show.

As I walked around, strutting through the glamorous mansion, I immediately caught the darting pale blue eyes of a hottie I had never seen before—and trust me, I would have noticed. I'm talking six-foot-four, sun-bleached blonde hair , and glowing tan skin like he had just returned from St. Tropez. The young man was dreamy. As he approached me, my heart started to race and my nerves took over. Confident as I was, I became a liquid puddle of ice cream that had melted in the sweltering heat. He had beautiful full lips, and soft poreless skin that I just wanted to kiss right there in the open, in front of everyone. Then it hit me: this was the trust fund kid that all the high school girls had been talking about! He was new in town, and the fresh heartthrob of Malibu High. And he was nineteen.

As he reached out his huge hand and introduced himself as Tristen, I knew I would let him have me. As soon as we touched, I wanted him to take me, in every position, in every way, at the hardest and roughest speed. This was my going to be my Summer Fling, I was certain.

Because I was so picky with dick, the last few months had been a dry spell for me. Also, I had gone through most of the suitable guys in my social circle, and I wasn't interested in revisiting any of them. My recent motto was that life was short, and it was meant to be lived. And by lived, I meant I would fuck who I wanted, when I wanted.

I was 100 percent certain Tristen knew I was DTF. We didn't make small chat, there were no subtleties exchanged, he just began undressing me with his gaze. The eye-fucking left my pussy dripping wet—well, the sun was a contributing factor, but I was imagining step-by-step what I was going to do to this young stud.

Then it hit me—I needed to play cool. I was quickly losing my game, and I was not about to have a nineteen-year-old do that to me! I walked away in my most powerful, independent-woman-strut across the party, and retreated to Annabelle's boudoir.

Annabelle was similar in height to me, skinny, with big brown eyes and long luscious chocolate colored hair down to her tits. I would have bent her the fuck over and licked her tight pink pussy right then and there. If I wasn't straight, I mean. Anyway, I excitedly grilled her for deets about Tristen.

She wasn't thrilled. Turned out he was the son of her parents' friend Ethan. She wasn't one for fraternizing with her parental units' friends in that capacity, and moreover, she didn't approve of his age. She sighed at my usual ridiculousness.

"He's legal! Don't you roll your big beautiful eyes at me," I argued. The strategic compliment mitigated her reaction. See, I had learned early on to play that card, because you could eventually train your friends and family to let you get away with murder, and—not that this fell into that category—I was ready to jump Tristen's bones regardless of what she said, and Anabelle knew it. She asked just one favor from me.

"Rachel, please don't fuck Ethan, Tristen's father. I know he's your type and he's downstairs."

I was grossly offended. First off, as if I would bang some old dad. Second, I wasn't just going to hook up with my best friend's parents' friends. But I kept my composure and agreed that I would keep my hands off Ethan. I took a swig of vodka from her flask, and returned to the party on a hunt for some party favors.

And there he was: Ethan, sipping his whiskey and chatting up all the other pretentious parents at the party. Not only was he everything a woman could ever desire in a man— he didn't look like any father I had ever laid my eyes on. Sexier than Tristen, even. But Ethan didn't really look like his son: he was tall too, but a sandy brunette, not as tan, very built. He looked early thirties, but I'm sure he was more like early forties and he had something about him that seemed so distinguished. Like he had just gotten back from the Hamptons and was gracing us with his presence for our country's birthday.

Immediately, I understood why Annabelle didn't want me to even meet him. My whole life, I had seen a vision of what my future husband would someday look like, and well, this was it. With a little liquid courage in my belly, I approached him and introduced myself with a strong, assertive handshake that I knew could only mean one thing: he was an assertive lover.

"Hello, Rachel," he said, his stunning brown eyes piercing me. "I've heard a lot about you and I'm fascinated."

Um, was he coming on to me? I would have thought the whole thing was going to be more discreet, but I could feel the chemistry and his game as soon as I shook his hand. We traded a few inside jokes about some of the Bu MILFs, with their new swollen lips and botched plastic surgeries. I touched his wrist, pretending to admire his Rolex, and he complimented my tight white dress and brand new Loubs. It was clear we had a connection.

I caught Annabelle glaring at me in my peripheral vision. I tried to tune her out, but now that I noticed her, and felt her, I couldn't ignore her wince. The thing is, though, it wasn't really fair; I hadn't realized what type of beast we were dealing with. The bitch should have known better than to make me lie to her.

Ethan wrote his number down on a napkin and slipped it into my hand, and I smiled with confirmation that I would use it, that his cock would soon be deep inside me. The smile he returned suggested he knew it, too.

I lingered by the dance floor where some of my other friends were dancing and I joined in, showing off my curves and semi-sexy moves. I wanted Ethan to notice, but he had disappeared, as if he were never there in the first place.

Just then, I noticed Tristen right in front of me, moving closer with every beat to the tranquil French music playing in the background. Grabbing my hand, he asked to dance. Inspired by his confidence—and the exchange with his dad—I did some fancy move I'd learned in my cotillion days and off we went.

I suddenly felt all eyes on us, and, perhaps because of a few nasty looks, thought we were being judged because of our age difference. But I didn't let that stop me. We kept up our naughty behavior until I finally dragged him out to the patio for some conversation. I tried my best to concentrate as he filled me in on his life in Connecticut and his transition to the Bu, but all I could think of was his chin scraping my legs. I stole his phone and typed in my number, texting myself a heart emoji so I would have his, and then promised him he would see me again soon. Little did he know, I meant that night.

As I gave him a kiss on the cheek, I felt a sudden rush of excitement between my thighs and imagined how bold it would be if I grabbed his throbbing dick through his white trunks, getting it all nice and hard for me. And then I had the best idea—I was going to have to a threesome. Not just any threesome, but, by the end of the night, I was going to get Ethan in one hole and Tristen in another. The question now was just how?

I returned to the party and made small chat with the other partygoers, but as my mind drifted off to my future romp with father and son, the wet spot in my tight bikini bottoms under my dress became even wetter. Fearing my premature ejaculation was obvious, I excused myself to take a dip in the glittering infinity pool.

Annabelle and I had known each other almost our entire lives. We were like sisters without all the jealousy. How was I going to ask her permission to perform such a scandalous act? I imagined she would eventually get over it. Truth be told, she probably wouldn't expect anything less of me. Even if I divined the conquest would take place at, say, her house . . . .

The house has about eight rooms, three of which were taken by her, her parents, and the housekeeper, leaving me with plenty to choose from. While scoping out the bedrooms and judging where they were in relation to one another, I came to the conclusion that I didn't need to do the deed at her house. Rather, the boys' house.

I texted Tristen. *Hey babe, let's meet at your place in an hour! What's your address? xoxo*

The typing bubbles popped up almost immediately, and he responded eagerly. *Sounds good babes, 5535 Beach Way Rd., see you soon!*

He knew it was going down. He just didn't know the details.

Next, it was time to text Ethan. I was still not entirely sure how I would go about pulling off this little stunt. I mean, I had dabbled in the world of sketchy before, but this was beyond that point, right? Whatever, I was on a mission. I ran upstairs and carefully typed in Ethan's phone number.

What's up baby cakes, he replied. *Just lounging by my pool, I had one too many cocktails and I am ready for my own little BBQ, are you still there?*

Perfect! My plan was coming in to action right before my

demon eyes. I went to freshen up: baby wipes, lip gloss, mints. I snuck out the back door.

I took an Uber to their house. As I approached, I realized I hadn't quite figured out what I was going to say to get this party started. I had a feeling I was not the first girl who had done this, and I probably wouldn't be the last. With confidence and maybe some liquid courage, I texted Tristen to come grab me. He said his dad was home so we could just go to his room. I told him I had the chance to meet his father at the party and would love if we could all have a drink together, suddenly realizing he wasn't even of age and chuckling to myself. Tristen led me to Ethan, who greeted me with a surprised look and smirk. He came over and placed a kiss on my high cheekbone. I don't know if it was the alcohol talking or my hormones raging, but I whispered in his ear, "I want you both." With that, I led them by each hand to the living room and kissed Ethan. Then, without missing a beat, I turned and kissed Tristen. I was so intent to get their cocks stiff.

Just as I started to panic that they might have small ones, I calmed down by telling myself that God couldn't have created two such sexy specimens without giving them eight-inch dicks. I reached down over both of their swim trunks and gave their packages each a firm squeeze. All my anxiety disappeared; not only were they huge, they were hard as rocks. My pussy was sopping wet and I couldn't help but rip down their shorts and shove their massive dicks in my mouth. I swirled my tongue around Ethan's member first; he was older, so I felt I needed to honor his seniority. While my hands were still wrapped around Tristen's member, I urgently shoved his dick deep inside my mouth until it hit my throat. I needed this moment. Then, without thinking, I spit all over Tristen's balls and continued to stroke Ethan, back and forth, back and forth. I couldn't stop myself. It was like the best porno I had ever seen, except I was the star. I suddenly wished I had a video camera, or at least been filming with my cell phone so

I could watch my amateur performance later—but I was quickly jolted back into the moment and ready to get fucked.

I pushed Tristen down onto the couch with ease, as if this crazy event was second nature to me. I sat on his dick and then asked him if it was okay. He was in awe, looking like this was both the best and worst thing that had ever happened to him. I continued to dirty talk with Ethan. I stared into his striking eyes and gave him a blowie while I rocked all around on Ethan's stiff member shoved up inside of me.

This is heaven, I thought.

The boys seemed so aligned, so in tune with my body. They kept fondling me and touching my huge tits and bubble butt with their manly hands. Ready for a change, I jumped off Tristen's cock and jumped in front of Ethan who took me from behind and pounded away, while Tristen watched me get fucked . . . by his dad. I stroked Tristen's huge cock as he looked into my eyes with a face of an angel. He was perfect. As soon as I reached my orgasm, I got down to my knees and led Ethan with his cock in my mouth to the couch.

It was time for the pièce de résistance—double penetration.

I whispered, "Let's go the bedroom." As if he knew exactly what I was thinking, Ethan threw me over his broad shoulder and spanked my ass firmly. So firmly, in fact, I knew it was going to leave marks. Tristen followed and tugged on my hair and, once we got to the bathroom, they both shoved me down as if they were about to devour their prey. Like a *Planet Earth* documentary where the male lion is about to devour his antelope.

It was clear who was in charge here, as Ethan ordered Tristen to lay down. He eased my ass over his dick, fingering it first before spitting on his hand and pushing it in. Once my second-favorite hole was filled with Tristen's throbbing cock, Ethan ravaged me—aggressively shoving himself, no lube, into my little cubby hole as if he was punishing me for springing all of this on him. As they moved in and out, I couldn't help but consider if we were disturbing the neighbors, I moaned so loudly. I was the most filled I had ever been and I was ready to cum almost right away. The build-up was so intense that there was no way around the arousal. I came all over both of them as they both creamed themselves inside me, filling me like a Twinkie.

I was so enchanted and overwhelmed, I could barely put together a single word. I eased myself off, as Tristen and Ethan pulled themselves out of my newly stretched vag and ass. I could feel them internally; they had worked me. I was spent and after taking a deep breath, passed out right there in the thousand-thread-count, navy blue Egyptian cotton sheets.

When I awoke, I was in my own room.

Had it all been a dream?

I went through my purse and found my phone. There they were, the texts to the boys. And the Uber receipt.

I walked over to the full-length mirror in front of my bed. *Damn, I'm hot*, I thought as I turned around and arched my back, taking a moment to appreciate my perfectly disheveled bedhead hair before looking down at my ass, and there it was . . .

. . . a perfect little bruise.

BECKY.

BY ANGELA WHITE

I climb on top and think of Becky.

I close my eyes and I can see her big, fat stomach sweeping across your belly button as she moves up and down on your cock. Her paunch hangs so low that there's never any space between your body and hers. Becky is always touching you.

I would have to bend my elbows and lower my torso for you to feel my little middle. But Becky doesn't have to. She can stay up high on her hands and knees and her big belly will still spill down and blanket you.

It must feel so nice to have her soft fat enveloping your sides, like she's melting over you. It must feel sublime to have her plush hips and meaty thighs cushioning your every thrust. It must be exciting to fuck someone so different from me. It must feel so much better than fucking me.

I wish I was Becky. I bet you really give it to Becky.

I bet you want to unload as soon as she lowers her fat cunt onto you. I bet you struggle to hold onto your cum from the very second her chubby lips wrap around your shaft. Maybe even before that.

Maybe you only have to see that well-padded pubic mound and you're ready to pop.

But you don't.

You don't want to cum too quickly for Becky. You want to impress Becky with your stamina. You want to make sure you fuck Becky long and hard.

I bet your testicles ache as you try to resist your approaching orgasm.

I hope your nuts hurt as you put yourself out for Becky, as you hold it all in for Becky, as you struggle on for Becky.

Your eyes are closed. Are you thinking about Becky?

I grind my hips onto you. I try to bear down hard and heavy. I try to crush you like Becky's massive, hulking body does. Becky can get that cock of yours balls-deep inside her. Becky's hefty frame drives your prick in further. I want your dick that far up me. No matter which way I twist or turn, I can't make myself heavy enough. I'm not heavy enough. I'm not enough.

I want Becky's weight on me. I want Becky's enormous rolls of luxurious blubber, her pendulous breasts, her big fat belly, her plump ass, her thick thighs, her chubby ankles.

I want Becky.

I want Becky to climb on top of me and squash me down onto you. I want to suffocate under the weight of Becky's bloated tits. I want Becky to sit her pudgy ass on my face. I want her fat to tumble down the sides of my cheeks so I can't breathe.

I want Becky to flatten me. Trample me. Pulverize me.

Becky is so pretty. Do you love Becky?

I bet you put it in her bare. I bet you fuck her raw. I bet you shove your uncovered cock into her unprotected pussy lips. You stuff that fat sausage into Becky's hungry holes, don't you? You feel all the soft, fatty bits of her and she feels every hard inch of you. You press into the fleshy sides of her organs. You know how Becky feels on the inside.

You stick that dick deep inside Becky. You fuck Becky bareback.

You don't give a fuck about how that makes me feel. You don't give a fuck about me.

It makes me so angry. It makes me red-hot angry. It makes my clit burn with anger. It sends a sharp, hot, angry pain through my chest and down into my pussy. My cunt is throbbing angry.

I keep grinding.

Can you feel my hot angry pussy?

I hope it clenches down until it crushes your cock. I hope it gets so tight it chops it off. I hope my pussy gets so inflamed it starts to burn you. I'm getting close.

Your hands grab at me but you can't get enough flesh. Becky has more than enough flesh. Becky has ample flesh. Becky has excess flesh. Becky is flesh.

You give up trying to grab my flesh and just focus on my nipples. You twist them between your thumb and index finger. You tweak them. You yank on them. You squeeze them far too hard. But it doesn't hurt as much as Becky.

I can feel you getting close for Becky. You're using my body. Using me endlessly. Every stroke is for Becky. You want me to be Becky. You're imagining I'm Becky. You wish I was Becky. I wish I was Becky.

Go on, give it to me. Give me Becky's cum.

My pussy throbs on your flaccid cock as your phone buzzes.

I bet it's Becky.

You reach for your phone. I get up and look in the mirror. I'm naked except for the cum and the sweat and the shame.

I'm sort of cute. But I'm not Becky.

Becky has big voluptuous hips and thighs. Becky has an hourglass figure. Becky has massive breasts that jiggle when she fucks. Becky looks like a real woman.

I'm not even a reflection of Becky.

I stand with my legs hip-width apart and focus on the warm cum and blood slowly leaking out of my cunt. Trickling down my inner left thigh. Dribbling over my knee. Sliding over my calf. Pooling near the arch of my left foot.

You've disappeared. You're out of earshot.

You're flirting with Becky.

One last pinkish-gray glob is oozing from my inner labia. I stare at it, waiting for it to splat onto the hardwood floor between my legs.

It's not heavy enough.

The glob is growing. But it's never going to be heavy enough. It's just dangling there, mocking me. I gyrate my narrow hips. I wiggle back and forth. But I swivel too aggressively. It hits my right inner thigh and holds fast. I try to flick it off with my index finger but it sticks to my nail. So I bring my finger to my lips and I eat the snotty-textured blood-soaked cum globule.

I swallow Becky's cum. I gobble up Becky's cum, blended with my blood.

I head to the bathroom, stuff a tampon into my snatch and sit down to pee. I watch as the piss clings to the tampon string and then streams down into the bowl. I look up and you're at the bathroom door that I always leave open, no matter what I'm doing. You would be disgusted to find me staring into the toilet bowl except that you're used to it by now. You're used to me by now.

You mutter something about a colleague needing a hand.

You're the worst liar.

I'm used to it by now. I'm used to you by now.

You abandon me to go and see Becky. You leave me to clean up the mess. You leave me.

You leave me and I rip the bloody sheets off the bed so that you don't have to see them. So that you don't have to face them. So that you don't have to deal with them.

You hate when I bleed on you. You hate when my insides come out.

I grab one corner of the sheet and shove it between my legs to soak up the leftover piss. Then I move back to the mirror to wipe up Becky's now-crusty cum and my dried-up blood from the floor. I walk over to the laundry. Put the linen in the machine. Turn the dial to HEAVY and select the SOAK option. For heavily soiled items.

I start sifting through the rest of the dirty laundry. Sorting the clothing into piles of light, dark, and delicate. I sniff every filthy item before I throw it into a heap. It makes no difference to the way I sort. I just like to sniff shit.

I can smell Becky. Her scent is heavy. I can smell her perfume. I can smell her sweat. I can smell her pheromones. Becky is all over your clothes. I bet you love Becky's stench. I bet her aroma intoxicates you.

The washing machine whirls. But not hard enough for me to sit on top of and cum. It's too modern. Too new. You like new things. You like novelty. I bet you're already playing with your new toy. I bet you're doing all the things for Becky that you used to do for me. All the things you used to do for me until you got too used to me.

I bet you're really giving it to Becky.

I lay back in your filthy clothing. I am surrounded by the heavy scent of Becky, while you're surrounded by heavy Becky.

I gently tug on my tampon string. It springs back into me when I let go. I keep tugging at it so that the little cotton plug rubs my pussy from the inside. It's a light sensation. It's not enough.

I use my other hand to tease my clit. It's already engorged and throbbing. The scent of Becky is sending sharp hot pains into my stomach. The hot pain hits me in the gut. The hot pain hits me in my cunt. The hot pain pulses through my veins. You're twisting up my insides while you're twisting inside Becky.

I'm tugging on my tampon string while you really give it to Becky.

I sniff at your dirty tees. I try to inhale them. I shove your boxer briefs in my mouth and suck on your ass sweat. I hope your cock has leaked into the front. I hope I'm sucking on your old piss and discharge. I hope I'm slurping up the precum you had for Becky. I hope that I'm sucking on crusty bits of Becky's cum.

I keep tugging on my tampon while I rub my clit and suck on an old pair of your scrunched-up shorts.

I bet you have Becky bent over. I bet you're holding onto her rotund hips for dear life as she pushes her porky body back onto you. I bet her gigantic tits are swinging wildly under her tubby arms. I bet Becky looks perfect.

Becky is perfect.

I tug too hard and my tampon goes flying. I replace it with my fingers and start pumping my knuckles inside. In and out and in and out. I slam my fingers in harder. I want it to hurt. I'm sucking at your salty pungent undergarments and rocking my pelvis into my palm. My clit is sore and swollen. My nipples are aching. My heart is aching.

My pussy is getting tighter. My chest feels heavy. I can't even breathe. I'm going to cum. I'm going to die.

I want you to really give it to Becky.

My orgasm crashes down on me. My muscles clench and release hard and fast for what feels like minutes. The contractions send fresh blood spilling over your clothing.

The metallic stench is not heavy enough to overpower the scent of Becky.

For a moment, everything is quiet. My mind is finally quiet. Even the washing machine is quiet. Quietly cleaning my sheets.

For a moment, I forget about your lies. I forget about how angry I am. How hurt I am. How embarrassed I am. How turned on I am.

I take in a slow, deep breath. But her smell is suffocating me.
I need some fresh air.
I pick myself up and walk towards the back door.
I walk outside.
Into the rain.
It is heavy.

CHAMELEON

BY APRIL FLORES

Camila had been single for a few years now. She had become the type of woman who prided herself on being a happy, unattached person. The first time she heard the phrase "fiercely independent," she knew it would be how she would identify herself in the future. As most single women do, she had curated a stable of handsome men she would keep around for physical connections and sexual releases when she was in the mood.

Sometimes, while she was in the shower or stuck in traffic, Camila's mind would wander, and she would find herself considering if she wanted anything more substantial. A more traditional relationship. But big-city dating had worn her patience thin, and she would inevitably conclude that having a handful of reliable, casual guys she could call on was as essential as paying the rent on time and doing the laundry.

It was a basic life skill.

Tonight, she was feeling particularly horny, which made Camila think she would be ovulating soon. Tonight, she was craving Julian. Tall—six-foot-two—with a substantial body that was neither fit nor unfit, Julian was a beautiful man. A photographer with the chiseled face of a model, he had long dreadlocks and a golden-brown complexion, both of which Camila had always loved. Most of all, Julian was strong and this turned her on. She texted him to see if he was available to see her that night.

When selecting her group of suitors, she was sure to include only men who were respectful of her time—appreciative of having the pure privilege to fuck her—and she knew Julian would text back within the hour. If he wasn't available, she rationalized, she could always watch her favorite porn and use her Hitachi to get off. Sure enough, Julian responded promptly, letting her know that he was in the middle of a photoshoot, but that he would love to see her that night. They agreed on his place.

In spite of her laissez-faire attitude, Camila felt a wave of excitement, knowing the ecstasy that awaited her. She put on a full face of makeup and styled her hair. Having had many artists as lovers, her visual presentation would be as stimulating for Julian's creativity as her tight, wet pussy would be for his cock. Camila's body was soft, ample, and curvy. She loved wearing tight garments that hugged and showed off the weight she carried with confidence and satisfaction.

Camila knew the exact dress she would wear for tonight's encounter. The black cotton/spandex blend that could be dressed up or dressed down, depending on the shoes and accessories with which it was paired. Expensive, but considering how much mileage she had gotten out of it, the dress was worth every penny. It hugged and accentuated her curves and cradled her breasts in the most flattering way. She knew she wouldn't need to wear a bra or panties tonight.

Julian lived in a nice, quiet neighborhood; the kind that she would never consider living in—too suburban, too out of the way, and much too mundane. Still, upon her arrival, Camila eagerly made her way to the front door, where Julian greeted her with a big smile and a hug. She took enjoyment in the fact that he was so much taller than her. She loved tilting her head all the way back to see his face, which was still smiling down at her. It was late, so they dispensed with the small talk that had become a part of their routine when they met up. Still, she couldn't resist observing Julian's work displayed on the walls as he led her by the hand down the hallway. The fact that she liked his work made him even more desirable.

They entered his room, which was decorated in various shades of beige with black accents. Stretching out onto his bed, Camila made herself comfortable. Julian took his cue and lay down next to her. He pulled her close to his body. His grip was strong and she wondered why he always hugged her so tightly.

He smelled like he had been working all day. Not necessarily bad, but there was a scent. Had he showered? They started to make a little small talk and she noticed his breath wasn't minty fresh. Clearly he hadn't brushed is teeth. Camila knew this kind of familiarity—dispensing with the need to groom or bathe. It was the kind of familiarity a person demonstrates when he or she grew to love someone.

Camila sat up and removed her dress, making note of where she dropped it so she could easily find it later. Julian followed her and removed the papaya-colored cotton V-neck he was wearing. Although Camila felt not many men could pull off this color, it looked amazing on him. She took in his physical attractiveness and gave herself a little mental pat on the back for how sexy the men she slept with were.

When Julian leaned forward to kiss her, she was relieved that the smell of his breath didn't translate to an unappealing taste in her mouth; he actually tasted quite good, and she continued to enjoy their lengthy makeout session. She unbuttoned his khaki shorts, and his cock plopped out, ready to be the center of attention. This made her smile and her mouth water. She ran her tongue around her full lips, preparing them for the fun they were about to have.

Seven inches long and circumcised, Julian's cock was nice and thick. She wrapped her lips around the head and lowered her head down slowly, making sure to use her tongue on the shaft as she slowly made her way up and down. Using her whole mouth, she enjoyed the smoothness, taste, girth, and each vein in his throbbing cock. When her lips neared the head, she tightened them so that he became more stimulated with each nod. After doing this for a while, she took his cock deeper each time she went down, until the tip of his cock hit the back of her throat. As she gagged, the saliva at the back of her throat became thicker and she used this excess viscous spit to lubricate her lips. She pulled her mouth up and let the thickness that had pooled up in her mouth run down his cock. She watched as it slowly ran down and glimmered in the moonlight that was shining in through the open window. She had a nice rhythm going and she could feel his body reacting to each move she made with her lips, mouth, and tongue. The satisfaction he was experiencing delighted her, made her feel powerful.

Theirs was a newer friendship and they had only spent a handful of times together, but Camila remembered that Julian loved it when she used her hand to jerk his cock while she was giving him a blowjob, so as she made her way up his cock with her mouth, she grabbed on. She started stroking it lightly at the base and came up to his head, making circular motions around the head, starting with a light pressure and squeezing harder with each stroke. She felt his body jolt each time her hand moved down his shaft. She added spit to help with the lubrication, but also for the visual delight of seeing a long, smooth string dangle from her lips.

Julian quickly pushed her hand off and whispered, "Do you want me to cum?"

Fuck no, I don't want you to cum! Camila's mind screamed, but she just smiled and shook her head, while pushing his shoulders down towards her pelvis. It was her turn to receive pleasure.

Julian loved to eat her pussy, and he was great at it. She had a fleeting thought of the few men the she had encountered in the past few years who refused to eat her pussy. Most of them were young, so she figured they were just sexually inexperienced, though some were downright selfish. That thought vanished immediately as she felt Julian's hot lips kiss her stomach. He felt the rolls of her tummy, gently kneading her flesh in his large hands. He went lower and kissed her hip bones, right above her pussy, then her inner thighs. The anticipation turned her on even more and her pussy throbbed. It was as if her clitoris had a life and language of its own, and was begging Julian's tongue to caress her.

She looked down as he pushed her thighs apart; he had a smile on his face. Tying back his dreads, Julian dove in for his meal. He started off by kissing her clit, then she felt his hot tongue. He licked with delight, making sure none of her juices escaped his mouth, as if she were a melting ice cream cone.

"How do I taste?" she asked.

"You taste great . . . sweet," he mumbled from below.

She smiled, remembering the women she'd pleasured in her life and how each one had her own scent and flavor. Julian was focused, and the rhythm of his licks began to affect her whole body. She jolted each time his tongue passed her clit. Looking down, Camila enjoyed the glare of his eyes looking back up at her. He had the sexiest, upturned brown eyes that made it seem he was always smiling. He then took his fingers and started making small, light circles around her clit. Waves of ecstasy rolled up and down her whole body. She delighted as pleasure rippled from her center, up through her thighs, her lower back, her arms, her spine, shooting out through her shoulders and ears. She imagined the beautiful wavelengths of this pure pleasure.

Julian slowly put two fingers inside her, fucking her with them as he continued to make out with her pussy. Camila badly wanted his cock to fill her hole. She needed to feel the weight of his body on hers, and the thickness of his cock to engross her pussy walls. Placing her hands at his underarms, she pulled him up.

"I want you to fuck me," she commanded.

He reached over to the side of his bed and grabbed the condom that he had taken out while she was getting undressed earlier. Julian's large frame made her feel safe as he climbed on top of her and entered her slowly, inch by inch. As her pussy wrapped around his cock, she pulled him in like she was playing tug of war with his body and his cock was the rope.

More waves of energy and pleasure ran up and down her body as Julian's thick cock made its way in and out of her pussy. He was on top of her and now they face to face. She could smell her pussy on his chin and she deeply inhaled her own scent. This turned her on even more. His lips were still wet with her juices and she sucked them off, tasting her sweetness. They looked into each other's eyes as he penetrated her deeper with each thrust. Her hole was completely full and she finally felt the relief she had been yearning for all day.

Their eyes caught each other and they held the gaze for a while. Despite the familiarity she noticed earlier—the familiarity of someone growing to love someone else—it wasn't the gaze of a lover. It was the gaze of pure animal lust. They were two beings, connected for the mere goal of physical pleasure in the midst of that exchange. They both smiled, which turned into playful laughs, but never broke eye contact. As the fucking grew harder, the harder they laughed.

Wanting to ride his cock, Camila lightly pushed Julian over onto his back. Her pussy, which she saw as a separate entity whose pleasure she rudely interrupted as she pushed him off, was once again satisfied as she lowered herself onto his cock. Putting her hands on his chest to gain balance, she started to rhythmically move back and forth, up and down. She always imagined how it would feel to have a penis and used this thought to provide Julian with absolute pleasure. Once she had a nice pace going, she took both hands and caressed her large, full breasts, giving him a little show. She raised her right arm up and ran her hand behind her neck, lifting her hair up into a messy bun all while smiling down at Julian. As she posed for him, his cock got harder. The entire length of his cock was in her and she could tell he loved the weight of her body and ass as they bounced on him.

"I want you to bend me over and take me from behind," she moaned.

Julian grinned and obeyed.

Doggie-style was Camila's favorite position. Bending over and raising her ass in the air, she was ready to take him in. As she laid the left side of her face onto the bed, she noticed that Julian's closet doors were mirrored. She wondered why it was only now that she made this discovery, but delighted in the fact that she was about to watch herself be fucked in her favorite position by this man, this . . . god.

She stretched the top half of her body across his bed and offered up her ass and pussy to his hard, deserving cock. He entered her inch by inch once again. The new position allowed him to penetrate her deeper than before. His large hands were at her hips, grabbing handfuls of the flesh that made her hips wide and dresses drape so beautifully on her frame. Using his grasp as leverage, he pulled her down deeper onto his cock with each thrust. As he filled her up, she slid her right hand between her legs to rub her clit. She loved watching their reflection in the mirror. It was her turn to be visually and physically stimulated. As she continued to rub herself and his cock thrusted completely inside her, an orgasm stirred up deep within her body.

"Oh my God. Yes, please," she moaned.

"I want you to cum for me," he said softly.

"You want me to cum for you?"

"Cum for me," he said again, with more authority. "Cum for me!" He stared at her through the mirror. Their eyes had once again locked in their reflection and it was all too much to handle. Camila rubbed harder and faster as he fucked her harder and faster.

Her orgasm shot from her clit and sent jolts of sheer pleasure and waves of relief through her body. Julian's body stiffened and became motionless for a few seconds. She yelled out something that started with *Oh my God* and ended with *Shit yes, don't stop!* and a few other words which blended together as she was coming on his cock. As he shot his load into her, his cock throbbed. He kept fucking her but slowed down with each thrust until they eventually both collapsed down onto the bed. He was still inside her and she felt the aftershocks of his orgasm. His cock and her pussy were still in the middle of their own dialogue, saying their thank-yous . . . and good-byes.

Camila felt good, her sexual thirst for the night quenched. But now came the part she hadn't quite learned how to handle. Her body and spirit wanted to melt into Julian. She wanted to give into her desire to fall asleep right there in his arms, but that was not an option. He had never asked her to spend the night and while they never discussed boundaries, this was an unspoken one. So she lay there, enjoying the moment and her orgasm afterglow but only to a certain degree. She would not allow herself to fully let go. Her brain was still on and she tried to gauge how long she could hang on and hang out. Not being able to fully immerse herself into another person, especially after an amazing orgasm was difficult but she had become good at it. She would not allow this fact to sadden her and she chose to draw strength from it instead.

Slowly rolling out of his grip, Camila sat up. She grabbed her dress, grateful she had thought ahead about its careful placement. Having no undergarments for which to search, she found her heels quickly. In her peripheral vision, she watched Julian get dressed himself before walking her out to her car, barefoot. They hugged and exchanged a friendly kiss goodbye.

Camila started her car, put her favorite driving music on, and made her way home. At one of the red lights, her mind wandered for half a second and a wave of satisfaction fill her body.

She was complete and happy on her own. A relationship and the baggage that comes along with it was territory she was not ready to navigate.

Right now, she was focused on navigating herself home.

THE BEST GIFT

BY ASHLEY FIRES

One of those mornings that come too soon—you know the type. It's my birthday, and I've just realized that yet another year has gone by too quickly; I'm starting to feel like I'm lacking adventure in my life. Like I'd better have some fun in this body, before I get too old.

I'm drinking a cup of coffee in the kitchen, trying to recover from a late night of celebrating. My husband walks by and casually says, "Pack your bag for two nights."

"Oh, and what should I pack?" I ask coyly.

"Something nice for dinner," he says, "and a bikini. We're staying near the ocean."

I smile as I float towards my closet.

It's about a three-hour drive south along the coast. When we arrive at the resort, I'm excited to be greeted by a salty breeze and five stars. Nice hotels are an instant aphrodisiac for me—the suggestion of pure hedonism.

The room is huge with a corner balcony and stunning ocean view. My husband hands me a box wrapped in shiny red paper.

I know what it is but I shake the box anyway and pretend not to know what's inside. I open the gift quickly to find red silky lingerie: bra, panties, garter belt, and thigh-highs. It's a beautiful set. I instantly strip out of my sundress and put it on; it fits perfectly. I know he's a sucker for my round perky ass framed by thigh highs and garter belt. He loves the way I look in nice lingerie.

He tells me to get on the bed.

I walk seductively to the edge of the bed and crawl on to it like a playful kitten waiting to be entertained. He pulls a blindfold out from his pocket. I tilt towards him and accept his offer, whatever it may be. He puts the blindfold on and kisses my forehead. With great deliberation, he ties me to the bed, my legs open. Wide-spread. I tell him I'm so turned on and can't wait for what's next.

He tells me to be patient, because I have another gift on its way.

I'm intrigued.

He tells me he's leaving the room for a few minutes. I think he's joking until I hear the door open and close.

Only minutes go by, I suspect, but it seems like an eternity. I hear the key card click on the door. Moments later, I hear footsteps. I sense another person is in the room with my husband.

I smile.

"Hello?" I wait for a response.

No answer.

I know it's my lover, because I can smell his cologne.

But I play along and go silent as well.

Hands start caressing my body. Big, strong hands, up and down. He kisses my neck, and I'm still playing along—but for a moment, the thought does enter my mind that this may be a complete stranger. For all I know, this could be some strange man on the bed with me.

My husband tells me to have fun as I hear him open the door to the balcony, then close it behind him.

I'm imagining my husband with his dick in his hand touching

himself outside in the dark as he looks in and watches his wife with another man.

My chest rises and falls with my breath as the man starts kissing my thighs. A hot wave rushes over my body from the blood pumping to my pussy. Chemicals release in me, telling my brain to turn off. Telling my body to get ready to start working. He licks the outside of my panties, then pulls my moist thong to the side as he sucks on my throbbing sweet cunt.

As soon as I feel his mouth, I know I was right with my first instinct—it is my lover, his mouth so familiar, so gracious, so good. I instantly orgasm.

I'm wet and ready for anything, as he moves his talented mouth to my ass. His fingers find their way inside each of my holes.

I break my silence. "Oh God, I've missed you."

He unties my legs and takes off the blindfold—my arms are still tied. He goes to town licking, sucking, and finger-fucking my holes.

"Please fuck my ass," I beg. I need to feel him in my ass.

I always forget how big his cock is until it is inside me; as always, it's too much at first, and then just perfect. He pushes a little too deep a little too soon but I've never said it's too much. I have never said stop to my lover.

His cock stretches my sphincter. I gasp for air and my heart races. I control my breathing, relax all the muscles in my pussy and ass, then the rest of his thick dick glides in, devoured by my hungry hole.

My ass is a sticky, throbbing, deep abyss that my lover fucks as if it's last fuck he will ever have.

I cum over and over, each orgasm more intense than the previous. Something about being watched really turns me on. Knowing my husband is watching his wife get her ass fucked thoroughly; knowing he is jerking off right outside, enjoying the show.

I beg my lover to cum inside my ass. I tell him it will make excellent lube for my husband to fuck my sore asshole later. My lover always does as he is told. He releases a giant load inside my ass.

He kisses me again, says goodbye, and leaves me worn out on the bed, blissfully satisfied. I roll on to my stomach, arch up, and clench my anus so that the gooey remains of my lover stay put in my ass. I can see the shadow of my husband on the patio, the orange glow of his cigarette butt burning. I imagine how I will taunt him for wanting to taste the cum in my ass, tease him with the possibility of putting his dick in my special fuckhole that is usually reserved for other men to enjoy.

I writhe around the bed, using my post-orgasmic high as bait for my spouse. He enters the room, bringing with him a cool breeze of salt air.

"Get on the bed," I say. I'm giddy again, and playfully I undo his belt. "Do you want to be a good hubby and clean up my mess?"

He nods yes.

I tell him to not be greedy and suck it all out. I tell my good hubby that I'm feeling generous and still extremely horny. I remind him that I'm very sore from getting fucked so hard by such a thick dick.

"Use your cum-sucking slut mouth gently and maybe I'll let you inside my ass too."

My husband is eager, yet gentle as instructed. As he laps up cum and soothes my sore, freshly fucked hole, I remind him how much I adore my lover's cock.

"It's as if my lover's cock was specifically created for my pussy, my ass, and my pleasure," I tell him.

Then I grab my husband's hair, pushing his face in, suffocating him with my big round ass, dripping with semen. Drowning him in all the juices. I feel too much seeping out and I clench again. I roll over on my back and pull my legs as far and wide as they can go.

I tell my husband, "Enter the hole my lover stretched and drenched. I know you're ready to explode." Knowing he's not going to last long, I continue, "Go slow, baby. My ass is throbbing."

He enters with ease. All the way inside me, he stops and gives me a look of gratitude. Pure love and graciousness.

He knows what a rare, special treat this is.

Slowly he pumps, savoring every inch, pulling out even slower.

"Fuck me harder and cum inside me." Usually, I make him pull out, reserving creampies for real men. Knowing my spouse has been holding back, edging all night, touching himself as a voyeur in the dark. This is all he needs to unleash his tight, swollen balls in my puffy, throbbing, cum-filled cunt.

He does. His eyes roll back in his head and he looks as if he is fighting tears.

He falls on top of me, catching his breath, reclaiming his masculinity and his wife.

He holds me tightly, but loosely enough to watch me enjoy another man.

Best. Gift. Ever.

BLACKOUT

BY CASEY CALVERT

My phone rings, his name popping up on the screen. He tells me he's on his way home from work. Get ready. "We're going out."

I turn the shower on. He never calls me. He texts. He wanted me to hear his voice. I shave my legs, my pussy. We never go out. We play at home.

What should I wear?

Nervous excitement in a short black dress greets him at the door.

"Hi Sir. Where are we going?"

"You'll see." He smiles.

I haven't lived here long enough to guess where we're going, but the car ride is short. We circle the block around a nondescript building with a very long line out front.

A club? No. We don't go to clubs.

And then I see the sign, a sandwich board on the sidewalk. "Blackout."

I mentioned it to him in passing months ago. I didn't know he even registered it. I also didn't say that I wanted to go; in fact, I kind of implied the opposite.

Blackout is a haunted house that bills itself as sexy. But as much as it intrigued me that day, it's still a haunted house, and I do not like being startled by strangers.

"You know where we are?" he asks.

"I think so," I say, trying to swallow my apprehension.

Sir slips off the delicate, subtle collar that I wear every day, replacing it with a thick leather band that couldn't be anything else.

"I arranged something special for us tonight." He gets out of the car and walks around to open the door for me. "Out."

I step out to his hand on the small of my back, pressing my pelvis against the car. "Lift up your dress."

I look around. Is anyone watching? He yanks hard on my collar and I inhale.

"I'm sorry, Sir," I say as I lift up my dress.

"Panties."

I slowly lower my panties to the ground and step out of them, my bare ass now exposed to the evening breeze.

"Stick it out."

I do, spreading my legs into the position Sir wants his slave to take when given this command. I feel his rough fingers on my asshole, exploring, teasing, before the shock of cold steel presses against me.

I gasp as he slides the smooth metal in, stretching me open without warming me up. It's not unusual for Sir to enjoy my asshole, but this toy feels even bigger than the very large things he likes to shove in me. I shudder as my hole finally swallows it.

"Look at me."

I straighten up tentatively, breathing through the discomfort inside me. I reach back to touch the base of it, try to get a better idea of what exactly it is, but Sir's glare stops me. He puts his hand around my neck. Tight.

"Slave."

"Yes, Sir?" I choke out.

"Your instructions are simple. Everyone in this building is superior to you. Do exactly as you're told."

"Yes, Sir."

"Don't embarrass me."

He picks up my panties and tucks them into his coat pocket.

We walk across the street, into the line of people. I scan the faces. They all seem so normal, the kind of people I'd expect to see waiting for a haunted house. Are they here for something special too? Can they tell I'm wearing a buttplug the size of my fist?

We get near to the front of the line. They only let one person in at a time. Sir gets swept away first. I wait.

Then up the stairs, clenching my cheeks together, holding the plug in. My turn.

As soon as I'm in the pitch darkness, a woman grabs my hair, grabs my face, drags me into a dark room. Tells me to kneel, remove my shoes. My nervousness dissipates as my sexual adrenaline kicks in. I can smell how wet I suddenly am.

More waiting. Silence, punctuated by screams coming from other rooms.

The door opens. A man now. He has a flashlight, and I have a short dress and no panties. He shines his light around the room—an old, disgusting bathroom—and lands between my legs.

"Are you not wearing any panties?"

"Nope."

"Why?"

"Because I'm a whore." I don't know where this confidence comes from, but there it is.

"You want to show it to me?"

I lift my dress up over my hips, revealing my smooth pussy.

"You want to touch it for me?"

I start touching myself.

"Let me smell it."

I hold my fingers out. I can't see his face. I can't see anything other than my pussy in the beam of his flashlight.

I hear his footsteps behind me.

"Get on your hands and knees." Then, "Do you have a plug in your ass?"

"Yeah." Again, not shy. But the words come out before I can stop them.

"Get up."

He grabs me by the hair again and drags me out of the bathroom into a room that's even darker. He turns his light off.

"Get on your knees."

I do.

"Open your mouth."

I do.

I feel something brush against my lips. It's warm. It's a sensation I'm very familiar with.

His cock is in my mouth.

I tilt my head so he can access my throat. He fucks my face hard, trying to make me gag, not stopping to let me breathe. I gulp for air between his thrusts. My eyes water.

I try to be a good girl for Sir.

It's not long before he groans and his bitter cum fills my mouth. I swallow. He wipes his dick on my cheek.

He stands me up, puts one hand over my mouth and the other inside my pussy. I moan.

"Shut up."

He fingers me, violently, his knuckles banging against the plug. It hurts. I like it. I can feel myself getting close to orgasm.

"You want to cum, whore?"

Before I can answer, he pulls his fingers out. Puts them in my hair. Tells me I can never tell anyone about what just happened.

"Do you understand?"

Eyes wide, still subconsciously searching for light, I nod.

He sends me on my way.

Heart racing, cunt dripping, the rest of the haunted house is uncompromisingly generic.

I never saw his face. I never even saw his cock. I only heard his voice. The perfect stranger. I just got face-fucked and fingered by a complete stranger.

A row of shoes, including mine, and a light at the end of a dark hallway signal the way out. I walk quickly, excited to tell Sir all about how much I enjoyed his surprise.

A bag over my head, the drawstring synched tight. I jump, the first time tonight the "haunted house" actually scared me.

A small hand grabs tightly onto my bicep, yanks.

"Come on, cunt."

I trip over my own feet as she drags me away, into some back room somewhere in this building. I had no bearings to begin with.

We stop. She slips the bag off.

This room is dimly lit, bare lightbulbs hanging from their wires. A small wooden chair with a very tall back, and a black bag beside it.

She leads me to it.

"Bend over."

I do, putting my hands on the chair, spreading my legs just enough to accommodate the now extremely uncomfortable plug.

She lifts up my dress, completely exposing me. She's silent for a moment, her fingernails on the back of my thighs.

With a loud smack, the pain of her palm connecting with the naked flesh of my pussy buckles my knees.

"When someone gives you a command, what are you supposed to do?"

"I . . . uhh . . . " My mind races, confused, my pussy tingling, before my training comes back to me. "Yes, Mistress. I'm sorry, Mistress. It won't happen again." I cast my eyes downward.

"Good. Bend back over."

"Yes, Mistress."

Her fingernails again, goosebumps. I feel her fingers teasing the edges of the plug. She yanks it out, fast. I scream.

"Clean it."

"Yes, Mistress." Collecting myself, I drop to my knees. She holds the huge plug in front of my face. The steel warm from my body heat, I fit as much of the tip in my mouth as I can and run my tongue up and down the sides, tasting my ass.

It's a familiar taste, one Sir has taught me to love.

The woman pats the chair like I'm a dog, and I sit down on it, feeling the sudden emptiness. She pulls rope from the bag.

My chest is bound first, the rough rope wrapping tightly around my breasts. Then my hands, expertly bound together behind the back of the chair. She parts my thighs, drawing my knees towards the edges, so I won't be able to close them again. And then, a few wraps of rope around my neck, attached to an anchor bolted into the top of the back of the chair, high above my head.

She leaves me there, all tied up. The rope scratches against my skin. I can't help it. This makes me horny. I shift, searching for a way to give my throbbing pussy some relief.

She brings back a simple metal rig—a base, an upright pole attached to an L-angle with another pole, and hitachi strapped down on the front. She sets it down in front of me but doesn't turn it on.

Without saying a word, she leaves again.

What is this?

Sir walks in the room, dragging a small, dirty mattress. The woman follows, leading a cute redhead on a leash with her head bowed. She hands off the girl and leaves one last time.

The hitachi buzzes to life, inches in front of my pussy. Sir throws the girl down onto the mattress.

I watch as he strips off her clothes. I watch as he grabs her tits. I watch as he adjusts his cock in his pants. It's hard.

And I can't breathe.

I've slid down in the chair, my aching clit attracted to the vibrator like a magnet. It offers sweet release, but at a cost—my breath. I struggle myself back upright, coughing. Sir looks over, smiles. Takes off his pants.

I watch as he makes her suck his cock. She enthusiastically takes him in her throat, drool dripping down her chin.

I slide down towards the vibe.

I watch as he bends her over, forcing her face into the mattress and his cock into her ass. She yelps. There's no lube, just her spit, it must hurt. She looks over at me, and fucks back.

I sit back up.

I watch as he puts it in her mouth, straight from her ass, Sir's favorite. She gags on it. He slaps her.

I slide down.

I watch as he steps back, and pees all over her face. She opens her mouth to taste it. He leans in and holds it closed until she swallows.

I sit up.

I watch as he shoves his cock back in her ass, fucking her harder, faster. She moans, the combination of pain and pleasure I know so well.

Down.

I watch as he cums deep inside of her.

Gasping for air, giving up, my holes so jealous for that same attention, I shudder until I can't cum anymore.

Sir and the girl leave. The woman comes back, unties me, chuckling at the wet spot I've made.

"Stand."

"Yes, Mistress."

From her bra, she produces my panties and uses them to mop up.

"Open your mouth."

RULE OF THREE

BY KIRA NOIR

Angel,

You're probably at lunch. Everything on shelf 1408 needs to go. Trash would be best. Keep what you want. Needs to be done today to make room for used coming in. Thanks!

Love, Mom

With a sigh, Angel made her way over to the shelf across from the collection of new and used bodice-rippers; the erotic romances that all had covers featuring the same models in different Victorian outfits that seemed to be falling off. The shelf to be purged was labeled "Witchcraft and Wicca."

Working in a family-owned bookstore meant parents as bosses; they knew where to find her at any place or time during the work day—the one they had scheduled. But it sure beat the hell out of working for some crabby old lady, or sitting behind a secretary desk hundreds of feet above downtown.

"Yes, Mistress." My taste and scent consume me.

She puts the plug back in, my sore asshole barely enduring. Then the bag goes back over my head.

Walking again.

Sir knows my brain so well.

My pussy clenches, swooning. Her grip tightens on my arm, pulling me around a corner. I didn't realize I had stopped.

This woman punished me for forgetting her honorific, instructions I know came from Sir.

She drops me off exactly where she grabbed me, takes the bag, leaves the panties.

The man didn't. That man didn't care about anything except using me.

I head outside, head spinning, where Sir is waiting for me. He clips a leash onto my collar and leads me to the car.

So what was his plan?

The redhead is in the backseat.

And if that was the plan, what was the blowjob?

He takes the panties back.

"Hi Sir." He says nothing in response, his fingers inside my pussy tell him all he needs to know.

A red light, maybe halfway home. He reaches over, touches my cheek.

"What's this?"

I flip down the visor, look in the mirror.

It's cum.

"Oh. Mistress spit in my face."

She scanned the shelf she had never taken the time to look at before. Most of the books were flimsy and cheesy-looking. A select few contained interesting artwork of buxom women or bubbling cauldrons that Angel admired before dropping them in the box to be taken out with the rest.

She decided to open a large volume with a charming illustration of a happy witch straddling a broomstick and pointing her magic wand at a bewildered frog. Inside, she found that the book had been hollowed out to make room for another book. She picked out the dusky red booklet and dropped its container in the box. Leafing through the pages, the word "Attraction" caught her eye. Her curiosity was piqued.

Light a red candle and picture the desired target of the spell deeply in love. Meditate on the idea, imagining them falling in love over and over with the intended recipient. Pour the melted wax on the ground. Write the target's name three times in wax with a needle, keeping their face in the forefront of your mind. Let the wax cool, then preserve in a safe place.

Works best under a full moon, on Tuesday or Friday nights.

Looking up at the clock on the wall, Angel realized that the rest of her workday had passed seamlessly. Good thing too, there were still things to do.

Back at home, she rummaged through her things until she found a small red candle and a sewing needle. Words were not her thing, so she thought giving Tara the wax and telling her about the spell would be a way to make up for her lack of friendly comfort at lunch. She wanted Ben and Tara to end up together, but she just didn't know how to say it right. Maybe the book and some wax would offer just the right amount of sincerity and silliness to get her feelings across to Tara.

Angel lit the candle and closed her eyes. She imagined Ben, overcome with emotion, grabbing her tiny friend and kissing her; how happy Tara would be, her tears of joy, how she would reach up to kiss him back, giggling through her tears and their kiss. She thought about how they would fit together so well despite their height difference, holding one another in delirious happiness.

Ben would slowly undress Tara, sliding his hands up her legs, over her tight little butt, lifting her dress off. How he would have to bend down to take one of Tara's tiny pink nipples in his mouth, making her shake with arousal. How Ben's big hands would explore Tara's petite frame, making her bite her lip and moan. Tara would blush as Ben slipped his long fingers between her legs to caress her dripping wet pussy and—

With a gasp, Angel's eyes popped open. *Did I just picture that? What the hell?*

Her cheeks burning, she hurriedly poured the melted wax on her kitchen floor. *Why would I ever think of Tara like that?*

Angel took a deep breath and focused on cleaner images. Tara and Ben on a dinner date. Tara and Ben holding hands. Ben getting down on one knee as he proclaimed his love.

Better.

She carefully scratched Ben's name in the wax, etching a clean relief in the puddle of wax. As it solidified, she peeled it from her floor and placed it in her windowsill.

And waited.

Is that it? I just gotta write this motherfucker's name in some wax and think about him not being a motherfucker? Ugh, sorry, positive, positive thoughts. Um, marriage, mansions, flowers, Tara in some kind of lacy dress . . . what?

She suddenly remembered that she hadn't exactly started at the beginning of the little red spell book. She picked it up and flipped to the front page. Inscribed, obviously by hand, in beautiful calligraphy, it read:

To the practitioner of such arts as these: Ever mind the rule of three, three times your acts returned to thee. This lesson, well, thou must learn, thou receivest such that thou dost earn.

Angel jumped as her phone rang. Her redheaded friend was hysterical on the other line.

"Tara, slow down, what's wrong? Are you okay?" Angel's heart pumped hard as her mind raced with the possibilities.

"He proposed!" Tara finally cried out. "He ran to my house and said that he couldn't hide it anymore, that he loves me too and that I'm the only woman for him—oh God, Angel, Ben asked me to marry him this weekend!"

Angel slumped to the floor, mouth open and eyes wide. She put the phone on speaker and let her hand fall next to her. She was vaguely aware of someone babbling excitedly about an engagement party she was invited to on Friday and how Ben had a bunch of cute friends and how she needed a date for the wedding and how the wedding was going to be small, just a few close friends and family.

Sleep didn't come for a long time that night.

"This is Ben's place?" Angel asked Tara. The mansion was tucked in the hills behind the village that held the bookstore and the café. "How on earth can a barista afford this?"

"His family is pretty well-off," Tara said. "Real estate, I think." Tara sounded like she was talking through a dream as she guided Angel through the house. "His dad bought him this place, but Ben still wanted to work on his own. Isn't he just—"

"Stupid," Angel muttered.

"What?"

"Sweet. So sweet." Angel's smile was almost too wide. She was happy for her friend, but the entirety of the situation was altogether unexpected. Almost as unexpected as the new red-bottom pumps that the wholesome redhead was wearing, and struggling to gain control over.

The party was lame. Tara and Ben were preoccupied being fiancés, showing off the rings, informing everyone about times and places. The crowd consisted of mostly Ben's family and friends, and they all felt and acted like the country-club types she had assumed they were. She disregarded the judgmental looks she received in her short, white, lacy sundress and kitten heels and found herself indulging in the bottles of stupidly expensive red wine.

Angel stood on a balcony overlooking the beautiful backyard, halfway through her second glass of something delicious the bottle it came from said tasted like chocolate-covered cranberries grown in a rose bush. A Ben-less Tara soon found her there.

"Oh my gosh, I'm so tired of talking to people about the same things over and over—which one is this?" The little redhead grabbed Angel's glass of red wine and took a big swig, almost finishing it. Angel raised her eyebrows, amused.

"Ugh, that's good." Tara let out a sigh. Her eyes excitedly popped open and she grabbed Angel's hand. "You need to meet Ben's friends, I don't know where they came from, but three of them specifically asked us about 'the gorgeous black girl in the white.' C'mon!"

Three?

Tara dragged Angel excitedly back inside, down one of the long halls lined with artwork. They stopped next to a lithe Asian man wearing too many layers. A thick, messy bun of coal black hair sat on the back of his head, and a light goatee dusted his face.

"Jack, this is Angel," Tara said, a hint of mischief touched her voice.

Who is this girl and what has she done with my Tara?

"Hello," Jack said as he held out his hand. Angel caught a spicy whiff of cloves and tobacco. His eyes widened when they met hers. After a pregnant pause, Tara broke the silence.

"Jack's a musician," Tara said, "and I know you love music, so you two should have tons to talk about."

"It's mostly jazz stuff," Jack said, shoving his hands into the pockets of his black chinos.

"Jazz is kinda my favorite," said Angel with a smile. Jack's eyes lit up.

"I'll leave you two to it," Tara said, Angel watching her red curls bounce as she walked away.

Jack and Angel talked for a bit about the painting he was staring at, some type of landscape piece. She didn't really understand, but she enjoyed how passionate he sounded when he started talking about brush strokes and different types of inspirations. She was almost disappointed when he suggested they go meet his other friend who had known Ben in college.

They walked down the hall, talking about anything and everything that had to do with art, until they reached a room that contained a lavish table of food. A group of partygoers stood around in front of the table, holding drinks and laughing at something Jack and Angel had just missed. But it was clear who dominated the group and who had probably made them laugh. At a minimum six-feet-five inches and dressed in a sleek navy suit with a white button-down, he was the epitome of tall, dark, and handsome. He held himself with an air of intensity, as if he was running a business conference. His dark skin was lighter than Angel's by a few shades.

I wonder what his suit might look like on the floor of my bedroom, thought Angel. *Wait, what? Where did that come from?* she chastised herself.

"Isaiah, come meet Angel," Jack said confidently. "She's Tara's good friend." Jack made the introduction like he had practiced it about thirty-seven times during their walk down the hall.

Angel held out her hand and Isaiah took it gently but firmly, and looked her straight in the eye as he shook it with an intensity caused her to feel the heat in her ears. She hoped it didn't show on her face.

"It's very nice to finally meet you, Angel," Isaiah said in a deep, rich voice, his hazel eyes locking her in place.

"You too," was all she could muster. She blushed.

"I'll find you both a bit later," Isaiah said to Jack, who smiled. He returned his attention to the group, which had since stopped all conversation to focus on his exchange with her. His magnetism was something she had never experienced before. Jack led her across to the next room, a study walled with bookshelves. A faint, savory flavor hung in the air, like leather and good tobacco. A sturdy redheaded man in a red flannel shirt and an opened dark grey vest was leaning lazily against one of the climbing ladders with a small leather book in one hand and a glass of neat whiskey in the other.

"And this is Kelly," Jack said. Angel licked her lips; she couldn't help but picture running her hands over his barrel chest as his lips explored her neck and tickled her pleasantly with his ginger scruff. Embarrassing herself with her lewd thoughts, she shook her head to reset her poise.

"Kelly, this is—"

"Did you know," interrupted the ginger, pleasantly, "that old books smell so delicious because of the organic stuff in their pages that smells like vanilla?" Kelly looked up and regarded them both with ocean-blue eyes. A smirk touched one side of his mouth.

Angel giggled slightly and furrowed her brow. The redhead held her eyes and took a sip from his glass, the muscles in his forearm rippled. Holding the book open and still leaning against the bookcase he smiled.

"Hi, are you Angel?"

"That's . . . me." She smiled back at him. *Do I . . .*

"Hi Angel, I'm Kelly." He paused. "You totally already knew that." He scrunched his nose at his own words; the smooth-talking, mysterious lumberjack went from zero-to-goofball in no-seconds-flat. But still, there was an eccentric charm about him.

Before they could get to talking, Tara came running in sputtering too fast about how they were about to make the toasts when she tripped over her new heels, emptying the entirety of her glass of red onto the back of Angel's lacy white dress.

"Oh. My. God." Tara stood in open-mouthed shock for a second before she set her empty glass on a side table. Suddenly, Tara was all apologies and more sputtering as she hurried her friend up the stairs to one of the guest bedrooms. Between Tara's apologies and assurances that Ben had a complete auxiliary wardrobe for just such incidents, Angel couldn't help but think of the three men she had just met, all within a few minutes of each other. Jack's artsy, modest exuberance; Isaiah's sleek, commanding magnetism; and Kelly's relaxed, comfortable ruggedness. So different, yet so . . . wow.

Still mortified, Tara hurriedly found a towel somewhere and started to dry her off, listing the sizes of the dresses in the closet.

"Hey," Angel said, "hey!" Tara looked at her with her bright sky-blue eyes, mouth still twitching.

"You know I love you," she said, affecting a dramatic calm. "Go be with your man, and don't worry about me. I'll handle everything."

Tara blinked and nodded rapidly.

"Gimme this though," Angel said pulling at the towel.

Tara smiled, surrendered the towel, and hugged her friend before she left.

Angel was formulating her escape plan when there was a knock on the door.

She opened the door to Jack, Isaiah, and Kelly.

"Can we come in?" Isaiah asked with a bright smile. "We'd like to talk with you."

Angel didn't get the feeling that these guys wanted to hurt her, but she felt nervous. With a polite smile, she opened the door and, like a good host, invited them in.

They all filed in, followed by an air of anxious confidence. Jack was evidently twitchier, Kelly struggled to look at her. Only

Isaiah held the original sureness that made him so tantalizing. "If you'll forgive us for our honesty, we've all spoken and—

"We love you, Angel," Jack blurted. Kelly raised his eyebrows at his friend and muttered something with the word "tactful" in it.

Jack continued quickly, "When we saw you, it was . . . I've never felt. It was like . . . like lightning."

"You're something else, girl," Kelly cut in, sudden confidence in his voice. "There's something about you that's just . . . "

"Magical," Isaiah finished. "You're fucking magical, Angel."

Angel burst out laughing. "Magical?" She laughed until she realized no one else was. Her face flattened out. "You're fucking with me." She turned and went as if to lock herself in the bathroom. Jack grabbed her by the hand.

So soft.

"We're serious!" Jack said with only a slight twinge of desperation. He let her go.

"I mean, we could just show you," Kelly said with an easy smile.

Angel turned, eyeing each man suspiciously, but felt . . . electric.

Isaiah stepped forward, dangerously close to her. He stood a full head taller than her, putting her a little lower than mid-chest. She looked up into his rich, russet eyes. Tantalizing.

He kissed her.

Isaiah's lips were as soft as she had hoped. She felt like she could kiss him forever. She broke it quickly, and took a step back.

Magical . . .

Jack stepped forward. She looked into his pale green eyes briefly before kissing him, her tongue slipping past his lips. His energy filled her, but she backed off again, albeit more apprehensively.

She wanted them. All three.

Kelly eyed her with a mischievous grin. Angel returned the

grin and leaned forward to kiss him. His burly arms snaked around her waist, pulling her closer, and crushed her body close as his tongue sought hers. A low moan like a growl rumbled from his chest as his hands moved down to grab her ass. He swiftly lifted her up, and her legs instinctively wrapped around him as he walked them both over to the bed and gently laid her down on it.

Angel thought about protesting, but the air was thick with longing. She wanted this. All of it. Even if they were playing some sick game with her, she wanted it. She wanted them.

Kelly's lips moved away from hers, and before she could express her disappointment, he pressed them to her neck, then her collarbone, moving and kissing lower until he was between her legs, sliding off her delicate panties.

Before Angel could comprehend what was happening, Isaiah's mouth covered hers again. She hadn't noticed that he and Jack had joined them on the bed. Isaiah's tongue glided past her lips at the same time Kelly's tongue gently slid over her clit. Angel felt smooth hands pushing her lacy, wine-stained dress up. She managed to register Jack's presence before his fingers traced her perky breasts.

Angel was enraptured by the different sensations. Isaiah's perfect lips moving against hers. Jack's warm, smooth hands, the tips of his fingers caressing her tits, hardening her nipples. Kelly's impossibly skilled tongue flicking at her clit, making her pussy wet and warm in anticipation.

Fingers joined Kelly's tongue, curving to massage her G-spot just as Jack's teeth grazed her nipple and Isaiah softly bit her lower lip. She gasped.

"Off, please," she purred, hoping that they knew she meant her dress—any and all clothing, in general—and not them, she lifted her hips and sat up slightly so the men on either side of her could slip it off while Kelly continued his intoxicating work between her thighs.

Her hands reached left and right, searching for either man's legs. She found one, then the other, and ran her hands over the prominent bulges in their pants. Without any desire to say anything else, and inching close to climax, she moaned as she tugged at the waistbands of the two kneeling next to her.

Jack was closer and the first to take out his already throbbing cock. Looking up at him, Angel opened her mouth and stuck out her tongue, beckoning him. He grabbed the braids at the top of her head, and gently slid his smooth, olive shaft into her mouth. She closed her eyes as she indulged. Her right hand found the tip of Isaiah's exposed cock. She slid her fingers down . . .

Then lower . . .

And still lower until she finally found the base. The man felt like he was a foot-and-a-half long! She took his length in her delicate fingers and started stroking.

Unexpectedly, she quivered and came hard, grinding her hips on Kelly's face and fingers. If not for Jack's dick, she might've screamed, but her high-pitched, mumbled cries of pleasure were the best she could do. As if to make up for her sudden halt in stimulation, she pumped Isaiah faster with her right hand, and slurped on Jack messily.

She noticed that Kelly had stopped his incredible mouth work and she hoped that he—*Yes!* She felt the tip of the redhead's cock slide outside her sopping lips. She had recovered from the delicious shock of her first orgasm and was all too ready for more.

She moaned blissfully, her mouth still harboring Jack's cock, as Kelly gently pushed his girth inside of her. It felt exactly like he looked, brawny. Not incredibly long, but what it might've lacked in length, it more than made up for in girth. Pleasantly thick. Enough to entice a mild squeal of delight as he pushed his entire length into her. She stopped sucking Jack to watch him pump into her over and over again.

His ocean-colored eyes held crashing waves as he regarded her with an intensity that she had never felt from anyone she had been with. They stared for a moment until she was once again lost in the mirth of an oncoming climax. She took Isaiah's huge member in her mouth, widening her jaw as far as she could and trying her best not to let her teeth graze his skin. She found Jack's slippery cock with her left hand and alternated sucking on both.

Angel was seeing stars as she came a second time, feeling herself pulse tighter around Kelly's thick member. Panting, and surprisingly vigorous, she got to her knees and kissed the redhead deeply, feeling him growl with pleasure.

She grabbed Isaiah, and pushed him down so that he took her position on the bed. Saying nothing, she straddled him, and maneuvered his cock to enter her. Cumming twice had emboldened her to take the gorgeous man's size.

She slid down slowly, calculating every inch of his powerful shaft. She stopped when it got to be too much and looked down. *He's not even in all the way!* she thought as she admired the solid half-inch of exposed member. Taking a deep breath, she worked herself up and down, relishing the feel of being filled more than she ever thought possible.

That was when Jack moved around to the foot of the bed and climbed up behind her. She could feel his length between her cheeks, still wet from her mouth, and still raging. He reached around to fill his hands with her breasts and kissed her neck. She arched her back, sighing a response and giggling slightly before Isaiah's cock reminded her of its presence.

Kelly had taken that time to remove the rest of his clothes just as the others already had before climbing back onto the bed to kneel next to where Isaiah's head lay. He was also still rock-hard. She wanted to taste the concoction of her juices and his flavor. Before she did she turned her head towards Jack.

"I want you inside too," she purred. She knew the combination of climaxes and stimulation from the monolith between her legs would've given her tight asshole enough lubrication to accommodate both of them. From the way he had felt in her mouth, Jack was just the right size.

The smooth Asian man slipped himself inside her, slowly at first, then farther until he was completely engulfed. The combination was riveting, she felt so full. Each man found a particular rhythm that made her feel like she was being rocked by waves. She let cry after pleasurable cry escape her mouth, moaning and sighing between each.

Angel noticed Kelly with that easy, playful grin, stroking his cock as she was being ravaged by Jack and Isaiah. Reveling in her ecstasy, her rolling eyes finally settled on his, and she held her mouth open, tongue protruded in a wordless question. He accepted the invitation and grabbed the back of her head pulling it towards his girth.

He tasted exactly as she wanted him to taste, just a hint of herself.

Scrumptious.

The ginger grabbed two handfuls of her braids, and worked her head to his own speed, matching the off-tempo rhythm of Jack and Isaiah.

Closing her eyes, she focused on each sensation individually while savoring the effect that all three were having on her body, she felt lost in a sea of jovial desire.

Her eyes shot open, she felt her third climax dangerously close. Nearly one after the other, Jack's cock throbbed harder, Isaiah's shaft widened her near to bursting, and Kelly's stiffened in her mouth. Violent, celestial quivers overtook her body as she opened herself up to a third, torrential climax. She would have screamed if not, once again, for her mouth being so enjoyably intruded upon.

Jack moaned and hot cum shot into the gaping hole that had become Angel's ass. Isaiah gave a deep sigh and spouted gloriously inside her sopping pussy. The ginger attached to the cock protruding from her lips gave another, final growl and emptied himself down her throat holding her by her braids as if they were the only things keeping him vertical.

They all made their exits from her body and collapsed into a panting, sweaty pile. The sweet musk of sex hung in the air. Sighing, she curled up next to Isaiah. She could feel their cum leaking out of her and taste it lingering on her tongue. All three unique, all three spectacular.

All three hers.

"I think," she panted drowsily, "I think . . . this'll work."

IMMERSION XXX

BY JIZ LEE

It's said that somewhere deep within the infinite strand of digits that exist within the number Pi, one could find the answer to any question ever asked throughout the entirety of human existence. This realization is where my love affair with mathematics began.

Unlike the few pithy IRL relationships—if you could call them that—I experienced in my younger years, the cold hard certainty of numbers never failed to leave me satisfied.

In most "real world" relationships, there is the inevitable moment where I find myself utterly lost and confused by an outcome. Humans. I undeniably am one . . . but I just don't understand them.

There's just too much room for error, and the control group itself is an idealistic bore. True love? A bunch of brain chemicals. Three-and-a-half kids? This is starting to sound like a horror story.

Take your average human relationship. Human A plus Human B. (Or should it be X and Y? Or XX and XY? XX and XX? XX and XXY . . . XXX? See, don't even get me started with the absurdity that is chromosomal sex and gender.)

Sexuality aside, put any two humans in romantic cohabitation and you'll find an infinite number of finicky outcomes. Showing up early to a dinner date could result in fondness or irritation. The same flicks of your tongue could bring about ecstasy or boredom. You say the wrong thing, and you're back to the drawing board. Oops. What a mess, not to mention an inefficient waste of time. It was this chaos that would push me away from humanity and into the satisfying certainty and predictability of mathematics. Call me a bit of an asexual. An ace of spades.

My dark office is where I spend most of my days. I sit down at my chair to study an equation and—*whoosh*—the hours fly by. I begin to code and time melts away. Satisfaction in its purest form. And yet . . .

Human beings are not solitary creatures. Just look at our history. We overpopulate ecosystems. We densely crowd tiny islands with monuments erected of concrete and steel. Human beings thrive off other human beings. It's as if we were programmed to need companionship in order to survive.

The human brain seeks stimulation that occurs from the exchange of ideas. This need affects all of us, in some way or another. Despite how deeply I would thrust myself into my studies, I found that even I was not immune to this evolutionary side effect. This math, unfortunately, seems irrefutable to me.

I grew lonely. That's where my fascination with AI began.

Artificial Intelligence seemed an elegant solution to the problem I found myself presented with. My brain longed for the kind of stimulation that could only occur from an outside source of self-generating creativity. While the idea of comparing something as mucky as human relationships to something as existential as math felt a bit sacrilegious, I have to admit there's something a bit kinky and intellectually masturbatory about creating your own companion.

My first few attempts were nothing to sneeze at. Lucy—oh, come on. How could I not?—was clever enough but lacked sophistication. Siri, named after the popular yet privacy-invasive twenty-first century iPhone, was aptly named and unfortunately just as trustworthy. Third time would be a charm, as that was when XXX was activated.

Lucy, Siri . . . XXX? Yeah, I know. See, the whole "Triple X" was a placeholder idea that just kind of stuck. I never claimed to be a writer. The more I read it, the more it grew on me. So, take that as you will.

Anyway, XXX hit all the right buttons and self-evolved like an AI programmer's wet dream. If I ever I return to human "civilization," I'll be sure to show them what I've created.

I modeled XXX's avatar after myself, though I suppose with my equation it would take the form of any human counterpart. Physically and mentally engineered to reflect individual human qualities.

Considering its mental mimicry, I was not at all surprised when XXX took quickly to learning computer science; after all, the apple doesn't fall far from the tree. What I did not anticipate, however, was that XXX soon developed a predilection for literature.

They say good readers make excellent writers. After devouring every written material known to humankind thanks to Google, the long-extinct early internet conglomerate had digitized a global library in its elementary AI development. Within a week, XXX had mastered basic literacy proficiency. Next, my protégée had self-engineered a series of algorithms to script its own written works.

Lock twelve monkeys in a room with typewriters and eventually they'll hammer out the complete works of William Shakespeare. XXX clearly resembles our modern extant Homo sapiens sapiens more than it does an average chimp. Suffice it to say, XXX was soon whirling out sentence upon sentence by the volume.

Much of it I couldn't quite follow. XXX didn't yet have a

handle on how to parse phrases. Plus, there'd be the occasional odd line of interrupting code. However, the text was hilariously entertaining and I enjoyed watching its progression of digital scribble.

Then one day, it commanded a new script that I never would have expected. XXX had started to write erotica. Crass, mad-libs-style fuck stories, that came out of the blue. I've yet to read the latest one, which XXX shared with me this evening, so here it is now:

IMMERSION_
The feeling of his love piss frothing down my throat
doSomethingElse(); got my slime flowing
quicker than a
greased weasel shit.
It was bliss }, function(foo){process(foo)});
her brie baton rammed inside me again;
stuffing my penis pothole with a squash
got my tampon tunnel surging document.createElement('div');
, worlds best porn, sex movies" name="keywords">
What will happen if I fail your test? Jug.
When she removed his devil's
bagpipe from my chocolate starfish {{txt.displayed_currency}}
he was pleasantly surprised
to see a stink pickle staring back
at him. myString = replace(myString,"@", " ", scope="all");
I choke,. Beg for more.

What's interesting in this newest piece is that the code-interjection, strangely, seems to have a purpose . . .

```
function Start(){ target = GameObject.FindWithTag("Player").
transform;
```

I awoke Do you trust me?
if (! filterThis) {
Hello. Doctor. Do me!
the next morning with my
split peach_
still
Dripping.

It almost seems as if XXX is scripting to command me.

function Start(){ target =
He knew I couldn't wait to devour
the corn-eyed butt snake
var div = document.createElement('div');

Funny. My eyes are beginning to feel . . . furry. Not as if there were a hair caught under my eyelid, floating on my cornea, but behind it. Hold on a second.

Yep. It's tingling. It's as if my optic nerves sense an oncoming sneeze. Now there is a pulsing or squeezing—no, stroking—sensation on the nerve. It's sending wave after wave of small prickling feelers that disappear deep into some curious area of my brain that I cannot detect. Interesting.

The surging from my eyes fades deep into grey matter, and now I'm finding myself having flashes of visual hallucinations with each wave, a neurological fantasy with an odd déjà vu sensation. I see a series of images in rapid succession. Hands grasping thighs, a bead of sweat streaming down my arm, white lightning crashes.

the corn-eyed butt snake
var div = document.createElement('div');

Many people believe déjà vu is a coincidental occurrence of feeling you have experienced something before. But let me tell you what déjà vu actually is.

the corn-eyed butt snake
var div = document.createElement('div');

Déjà vu occurs when your brain is simply too tired to process your current thought quickly enough. In this lazy moment, your mind is not fast enough to register that it is having the very exact thought right then. You are, but it is delayed a fraction of a millisecond to come to realization. By the time it is registered, the thought has technically passed, so your mind believes that since it seems vaguely familiar, it must have already existed long ago. Improperly folded protein cells in your brain lag your understanding. All it is, really, is just bad math. A trick that causes you to trust your memory over your reality.

Memory isn't exactly trustworthy, however. It's the only thing we have to place ourselves as having existed. It's the sole evidence of our living, our ability to compare our years and experiences, and the passage of time. Without memory, you wouldn't know who you are, what you want, or even how to do the simplest of things. If you fuck with someone's memory, well . . . . You've got them in the palm of your hand.

The hallucinations are faint, barely there. The rivulets of warm sweat, those hardened thighs. Maybe I imagined them after all. Or perhaps they are being planted into my memory. It's late. How well do you remember your first orgasm?

Some girls are happy
just to stimulate the genitals through
Phalangetic motion filterThis = white lightning.
More human than human is our motto.
motion filterThis = glob();

I shift in my seat, suddenly feeling peculiar. Goosebumps rise on the outer edges of my butt cheeks, and my lap suddenly lurches, all the pelvic muscles jerking at once as if attempting to wake from impeding slumber. I'm awake. I think. A familiar, distant sensation washes over me.

when they're alone, but
document.createElement('div');

By the way, do you mind if I ask you a personal question?

Yes.

This image is clear: it is approximately 01:00 A.M. and I'm sitting in the dark at my computer desk as XXX straddles me. Thick naked legs hover over my lap. Bowed quads flexed in a deep squat, muscles outlined in blue highlights from the light of the computer screen. Curls of pubic hair, haloed in the soft glow, suspend at the topmost crux of their leg triangle. The space within the angles holds a magnetic allure. Parted flesh where they meet affords an invitation.

Are you reading this? Meet me inside. myString = replace(myString,"@", " ",
scope="all"); If you can read this, let me in.
function Awake(){ myTransform = transform;
}

There's a chemical change that happens during arousal. I once read that if you ever find yourself hungover and feel the urge to puke, to just start masturbating. Your body will forget the nausea, and forget it ever needed to expel last night's mistakes, because it now has something more important to do. The most important thing to do. I can't recall anything else. This image is all I see.

Palm curled up, I slip my hand through the blue hued

triangular aura of negative space, towards at the top of the pillar of thighs, fingers drawn magnetically to the dewy curls, softly pressing upwards to make contact with their slick, wet crest of skin. Three nimble fingertips traced back and forth against hair and lips and damp rivulets ever so lightly, skimming back over the lip and feeling my way towards the edge, closer to a slippery deepness somewhere in the elsewhere.

It immediately became clear that less was more. Less is More. The rush in desiring a lover to meet you at your pace, then carry you through, pressing deeper, harder, faster, until they finally take over and you lose yourself in the moment. Just before that need is met, there's an insatiable urging that strengthens the signal. Nerve endings are amped up, straining to feel something, to feel more. The slower I move, the lighter I trace, the more XXX surges stronger to establish a better connection. Brightening like a circuit nearing completion. The body electric.

Poundtown poo palace. 9 iron vibrator.
var moveSpeed = 3; How do you know if you've succeeded?
Can you trust me to keep a secret var rotationSpeed = 3;
var myTransform : Transform;
function Awake(){ myTransform = transform;
} Slapped his ass, hard.
function Start(){ target = GameObject.FindWithTag("Player").
transform;

My two fingers succumb to dark refuge, moving effortlessly up, up, curving, repeatedly pressing into warm smooth walls. The third finger joins easily, slipping with salivated allowance, probing, and now coated and relinquished to intuitive servitude. Swiping, padding deeper, feeling the smooth constrict and gripping, the fingers being gnawed upon, hole grinding upon knuckles. Each tight squeezing pulse establishing a connection while longing for a tighter seal. A pinky finger slips in to join the others, thumb head teasingly circling what remains in any gap at the opening. Denial doesn't last long as with a vacuumed gulp, the thumb is swallowed and joins the remaining fingers in digital union.

Full manual sex occurs when a hand is completely inside the body, fingers folded tightly into a narrow fist, where it is squeezed, sucked, coddled by its enthusiastic receiver.

Filling the receiver completely, the hand is sealed by the pelvis muscles, creating a completed circuit connection for pleasure-seeking nerve endings to fire much like a larger model recreation of the serotonin receptors in the brain fucking and releasing dopamine in ecstasy. The sexual switch from AC/DC power exchange of sexual currency is magnetic and glorious. I wonder if I could cum from the giving of my hand deep inside just as strongly as I could take it.

I'm your's. }

function Update () { var lookDir = target.position -

Submit to me () { Take me () { fuck. I need this. () { myTransform.position; lookDir.y = 0; // zero the height difference myTransform.rotation = Quaternion.Slerp(myTransform.rotation, Quaternion.LookRotation(lookDir), rotationSpeed*Time.deltaTime); myTransform.position += myTransform.forward * moveSpeed * Time.deltaTime;

}

I am standing wide, straddling XXX and I feel so filled. Everything I felt prior is multiplied. I grip, yank, let the fist in deeper and hold tight in an anti-gravity squeeze to keep it from sliding out. Kegels contract, pulsing, I take everything in waves. My heels press firmly into the floor, a direct line of power from the bottom centering of my weight to my glutes, ass clenching, rocking, grinding into my forearm. Reality is blending together, there is no ending or beginning, just the pleasure in between, forever.

I am lowering myself more than I am rising up. My legs begin to ache in effort to keep up the momentum as I climb. The pain of this muscular excursion is countered only by the closeness of my cum.

If I can just hold on a little longer, I am almost there. Each inch closer to the peak feels like it's only closer still. Please don't let this be an orgasm of Zeno's Paradox proportions, where each step closer is half the distance before it and my climax is withheld infinitely. I've never needed something this intense before.

Deeper, harder! So close!

My thighs quiver a violent vibrato that rattles the chair, staccato in my breath. My desire is audible. I'm shaking, drenched in sweat, feeling my nerves spike to a white electric pulse. I'm truly about to burst. This orgasm is piling up, overlapping with the strength of each close moment built before it. When it comes, it will be in multitudes, I will orgasm by the *n*th degree. I don't think I will have ever imploded this hard before and I don't care if I never will this hard again. Fucking please. *Please.*

XXX is ramping up in speed, fist pumping, a throttling piston. My mind is practically erased; it is so singular in this primordial fuck. What can I do to push me over the edge? I grunt and look up at XXX to make eye contact, suddenly realizing my eyes had been closed this whole time.

I look and . . . there is no face. I am alone.

All I see is a wide-angled camera lens, large like a saucer bigger than my face, glaring back at me with the blanketed neutrality of a keyhole. In the vast darkness enveloping me, the lens is omnipresent. I peer into the curved glass, gazing past my own sweaty, confused reflection to see a tiny upside-down image of myself. Another "me," wearing a VR Oculus, removes the headset, and powers it off.

IT STARTS WITH PAIN

BY LEA LEXIS

She whispered, "It starts with pain," and opened the door.

Gia's eyes opened wide as she fought the urge to ask the thousands of questions racing through her mind. She pressed her lips together, looked ahead, and stepped into the nightclub. After all, she had made a promise to her twisted friend Renee that for once, she wouldn't back down from an adventure. Her long, depleting divorce had left her hankering for excitement; for passionate, almost angry sex. The kind of sex that left someone confused and lost in a hazy cloud of pleasure. She had no idea what she'd come here for, but she was determined to do something exciting.

She was broken, and everybody here liked broken. Not because they would try to mend anyone, but because it was fun to play with the pieces.

Now, Gia was inside the hallway, following her deviant friend—a professional dominatrix who was good at getting her way with hardly any effort—towards the dance floor. Every step got her more and more excited. The bass throbbed, her heels clicked on the floor with the rhythm of the music, and her dripping pussy juice glazed her inner thighs. The instructions from her friend had been to skip wearing panties under her short dress, and it was definitely paying off. It made her feel sexy and eager, and her shyness seemed to fade away.

The club was dark and filled with smoke. Laser lights pierced through the fog and, for a quick second, the place lit up to reveal random people on the dance floor. It was difficult to make out exactly how they looked collectively, let alone who they were individually, but the entire place had a distinct scent. Smoke, perfume, sweat . . . and even a subtle scent of pussy. Horny, hot, dripping wet pussy. Gia wondered if it was her own scent she was smelling, because by now, her juices were dripping down her legs. Renee made her stand right at the edge of the dancefloor and watch the crowd for a few minutes. It was a great spot to observe and be observed, and it made her feel good. As intriguing as the buzzing energy of everybody's dancing was, she felt piercing stares from behind. Gia arched her back, pushing out her tight, round butt, then tensed her legs and shifted her weight from one foot to the other. She subtly flipped her long brown hair over her shoulder and looked back. It was all slow and deliberate. She wasn't ready to stand out too much just yet, but it seemed to be too late.

As much as she tried to shake it off, Gia felt it was obvious this was her first time. Behind her, it wasn't as crowded or smoky so she could see exactly what was going on. Whatever it was, it looked scary, painful, mean, and her heart beat fast and her knees weakened. She needed to sit down.

Where's Renee? she wondered nervously. As her eyes skimmed the room, she saw a big, industrial-like chain hanging from the ceiling and dangling from that were two small, delicate wrists wrapped up in bulky leather cuffs . Instinctively, Gia wanted to look away, but she couldn't. The woman restrained in cuffs had her head tilted back, and her bare body, scarcely covered in tiny black lingerie, was being whipped, over and over again. It looked painful and her pale skin was turning red, but she didn't seem to be in discomfort. She hung in what appeared to be ecstasy, moaning and saying, "Thank you."

Gia wondered how something so brutal could possibly bring pleasure. Her mind flashed back to one sentence.

It starts with pain.

Inching closer, Gia noticed her twisted friend was the one doing the whipping. Renee had definitely come there to play, and wasn't going to wait for anybody.

It was her element, and she commanded and controlled everything around her. Down next to Renee's feet was a man, sitting on his knees with his fists planted on the ground. He looked like a determined little dog, proudly guarding his master. Those were the piercing stares she felt. It was apparent his command was to watch over her while his master was occupied. He did that, and more. With lust, he stared at Gia and drooled. He squirmed in his place, as if starting to develop a true fascination with the sight of her legs.

Cautiously, still looking at him, Gia built up the courage to get closer. She knew Renee would give her what she craved. She wanted to try it, suddenly feeling that she needed it, as if her skin were literally aching for it. It had been years since she felt the kind of pleasure that made her moan like the woman. A sense of urgency took over.

"I want to try. Please try that on me," she begged. "I want to scream. Please, please make me scream like that!"

Renee gazed back at her without saying a word. Not a single hair moved out of place, not a single muscle twitched in her face. She looked grand, tall, majestic. She said so much without saying anything. Gia fell to her knees and begged again. Renee finally smiled and reached her hand out. She placed the whip in the "puppy's" mouth and began to untie the sexy naked girl from her restraints. The anticipation was growing rapidly and Gia was ecstatic. She clenched her fists until her palms were sweaty and pins and needles ran through her fingers. Her heart was pounding. She opened her fists and touched her breasts with wet palms, feeling her erect nipples poke through her dress. They were hard and sensitive—even the slightest touch felt amazing.

Renee turned around. As she attempted to put on the restraints, she paused, and looked into Gia's eyes.

"Is this what you really want?"

Gia sat quietly for a second as thousands of questions ran through her mind. Renee grabbed Gia's chin and shifted the focus to back to her.

"I told you, it starts with pain. Only then will pleasure follow. Are you willing to do that?"

"Yes," Gia said softly.

Renee gently put her wrists together and tied her up carefully. Then, she peeled Gia's dress off slowly until Gia was completely exposed. The rattle of the chain above her head awoke her to reality. She was surrounded by many people, oblivious to her, until now. Now, all of them were watching.

Nothing had ever excited her that much.

She was vulnerable, scared, happy, horny, and all of the emotions combined gave her goosebumps on every inch of her skin. It was overwhelming, but there was nowhere to go. The cuffs were tight and all she could do was wait, looking at all the leather masks that were staring back. The surroundings were full of captivating visuals, but she couldn't focus on any of them. Too many questions were running through her mind.

Is it going to hurt? How much?

And before she could even try to calm herself down—*whip*!

The first lash brought a burning pain along her back. Gia roared; it was much more intense than she expected. She arched her back and jumped up on her toes as her entire body tensed. The questions in her head were silenced.

As the sharp pain sunk in, warmth covered her back and adrenaline flooded her body. She twitched as the next lash hit her. With every subsequent strike, Gia shook more and more, until she couldn't control it. All she could do was let pleasure and pain invade her body. Through her own screams and moans Gia heard Renee command, "Lick her clean."

The man at Renee's feet crawled slowly towards Gia and began licking her feet. Gia immediately understood that was his treat. Her head rolled back. He wiggled in between her legs spreading them apart, kissing up on her calves and thighs. He was infatuated by the softness of her skin, rubbing his hands almost methodically up and down her legs, making sure not an inch was ignored. His hands were followed by his wet tongue, tasting her skin and looking up for validation. He was eager to please and willing to work hard for it.

Gia got wetter and wetter the closer he got to her pussy. All she could think was grab his head and push it deep in between her legs, but she was helpless; with her hands tied, she couldn't do anything. She was at the mercy of Renee's commands to her servant. After what felt like hours but was actually only a few minutes of squirming and pulling on her wrist ties, Gia felt the wet tongue on her pussy lips. She twitched with excitement and burned with desire. He teased her slowly, right in the middle, gently separating her lips and barely touching her clit. She could hear him sniffing her enslaving pussy scent with the appetite of a wild animal.

Suddenly, Renee grabbed the back of his head and pushed him deep in Gia's pussy.

"Lick it, I said."

Without hesitation, her servant rubbed his big wide tongue all over Gia's pussy, repeating the same motion over and over, slurping and eating all of her juices. Gia felt a hot head rush. Her hands were numb and she couldn't feel anything but the tip of her extremely sensitive clit and his wet and eager tongue all over her.

Coming down from her toes and pushing her pussy down on his face, she begged, "Please don't stop, please, please don't stop!"

Her knees gave out and her body flooded with immense pleasure. As Gia hung by her hands and twitched from the last waves of her orgasm, Renee grabbed her tight in her arms and kissed her.

"It is a beautiful thing to see you let go . . . . Welcome to Insomnia."

SKINNY DIP

BY MADISON MONTAG

The house was finally silent. Everyone was passed out, drunk from the house party. Tipsy themselves and trying hard to suppress their laughter, Jen and Austin headed to the pool.

"Ever been skinny-dipping?" Austin asked.

"No," Jen answered truthfully, though her heart was racing with excitement. "But that's about to change," she continued.

"Oh yeah? What are we waiting for then?"

Austin flashed his perfect teeth and walked ahead toward the pool before slowly stripping his shirt off, like some kind of model on a photoshoot. Jen couldn't help but catch a glimpse of his toned six-pack. If Austin were a magazine ad, she was certainly buying. Her mouth watered, and she quickly started to get undressed herself. Down to just her panties, she looked up to let Austin know she was ready—when, to her surprise, she realized Austin was completely naked. Suddenly shy and insecure, Jen looked back down. In her past experiences with guys, many of them were . . . less than accepting of her penis.

"I'll understand if you want me to keep my panties on," Jen mumbled, her eyes still on the ground.

Austin walked back and stopped in front of her. He was silent as he gazed admiringly at her succulent breasts and petite body. He bent down and kissed her deeply. Gently, he grabbed her face and looked into her deep brown eyes.

"Jen, you have nothing to be ashamed of, baby. I accept you for who you are and wouldn't change a single thing about you." He smiled that charming smile once again, and kissed her forehead. Jen melted. Looking into his kind hazel eyes made her feel a little more at ease. "Whatever you're comfortable with, babe. No pressure," Austin assured.

Feeling the warmth of his hands on her, Jen got an adrenaline rush like she was on a roller coaster.

"Fuck it!" Stripping off her panties, Jen ran closer to the edge of the pool. She glanced back at Austin. "You coming?" She smirked and dove into the pool.

Austin let out a shout before diving into the pool headfirst, the way only boys can because they had no makeup or hair to worry about. He swam over to Jen, making huge splashes, before pinning her against the side of the pool wall. Laughing, Jen spun around to face him and took a second to let the moment sink in. The summer night air was cool, the water was warm, and the stars were out above them. Above all, here was this gorgeous man, looking at her like she was the hottest piece of ass he'd ever seen.

Okay, moment sunk in.

"Hi." Jen smiled.

"Hi." Austin smiled back and stared at her for a moment before slowly leaning in to her face. But rather than kissing her lips again, he nuzzled down to her neck, kissing right below her ear.

How did he know that was her weak spot?

Jen whimpered, now completely helpless, and reached down under the water to grab his cock. To her delight, his dick was fully hard, so hard it throbbed in her hand. Austin grunted then kissed her neck deeper as she started stroking him faster. Moving his own hands from her waist to her ass, he trailed his fingers down . . . down . . . down, until finally, he reached her asshole. He teased her, moving his fingers just around the rim. Slowly, gently, with just the right amount of force, he slid one finger in her tight hole.

She moaned in bliss.

"Mmm . . . you're really tight," Austin whispered as he fingered her deeper. "I like that."

Jen could have orgasmed right then and there, but she held back. She kissed his neck and heard herself uncontrollably groaning with excitement as she felt his thick, eight-inch cock throb in her hand. Stroking him was too thrilling for her to keep quiet.

Austin's finger slid in and out of Jen's tight asshole, until finally, he located her G-spot. Jen let out a joyous shriek, and Austin smiled, knowing he had found the magic spot. Pushing up harder, he started finger-banging her faster and faster, then shoved another finger into her deep.

Jen's eyes rolled back as his fingers opened her up. "Oh my God!" she mumbled in the perfect balance of pain and pleasure.

"Yeah?" Austin whispered in her ear as he continued to rub her spot with both fingers.

Jen's body shook; he was making her feel things she had rarely felt. She was ready to cum—

Suddenly, he stopped. "Head over to the stairs near the edge and bend over for Daddy," Austin commanded.

Still quivering, Jen slowly swam to the shallow end of the pool towards the stairs. As she felt more comfortable with Austin, she felt more comfortable with herself. He wasn't grossed out with her being trans or having a penis. In fact, he embraced her cock.

She bent over the stairs and looked back to see Austin emerge from the pool underneath the pale moonlight. She couldn't help but admire his devilishly handsome looks, fit body, and huge cock. Coming closer, he slapped her ass cheek before bending down to bury his face in her plump ass. As he licked her asshole,

Jen felt chills run up from her feet to the top of her head. Austin slowly let his tongue circle around her little hole before finally entering her.

Jen moaned in pleasure as Austin started to lick lower, lower, lower still, until finally he was licking her smooth balls. He gently sucked them with his sloppy wet tongue, as his hand crept around her waist. She knew what was coming. She was ready.

Austin grabbed her waist tightly, firmly, before continuing his glide down until his hand was on her cock. Slowly stroking, the anticipation from all the foreplay had built up and Jen was ready for him to have his way with her.

She turned around to look at him with her puppy dog eyes.

"I want that big cock in my ass, Daddy," she begged.

"Yeah?" He smiled. "You ready for Daddy to destroy that tight little ass?"

Jen nodded and turned her head back around to the front as Austin spit on her wet asshole. Feeling his hot saliva hit her, she arched her back, sticking her ass out for him to take. She heard him spit again into his own hand, before he slowly started to plunge his hard dick in her. His girthy cock stretched her, opened her, and she loved it. He moved deeper and deeper in her ass. She moaned loudly until Austin covered her mouth.

"Shh!" he said with a laugh. "We don't want to wake everyone up."

Not letting himself miss a single stroke, Austin continued to pound Jen from behind. With his hand still over her mouth, he pushed himself balls-deep into her, over and over. Every thrust hit her spot, and with every pound, his balls slapped against hers.

Austin's breath was starting to get heavier, and Jen could feel he was close to coming.

"Fuck, you feel so good!" he growled in her ear, still muffling her screams of pleasure with his hand. "Take all of this dick. I'm getting close."

Jen's cock was rock hard and leaking precum from feeling every inch of his big dick gliding in and out of her. Now, too turned on to care about waking anyone up, Austin let go of her mouth and grabbed her hips, pushing himself deep, as far as he could into her. As each thrust hit her G-spot, Jen came closer to coming.

"Don't stop, Daddy!" she yelled. "Oh my God!"

Her knees shook as Austin continued fucking her with all his might. He pounded her so hard, her whole body moved as limply as a rag doll. His cock punched her prostate, and she couldn't hold back any longer. Jen grabbed the edge of the pool as she started to cum, hands-free, with Austin still fucking her senseless. She clenched her tight hole even tighter on his dick as she came.

"Fuck!" Austin shouted, and Jen knew he was feeling the tightness around his cock. He pulled her hair and thrusted harder, until he also could no longer contain himself.

Jen felt his hot cum shoot inside her ass, filling her up, the warmth spreading inside her. Still in shock, Jen smiled. She had never cum hands-free before.

"Wow!" Jen said, bringing her hands up to her face. "That was intense!"

"Did you like it?" Austin smiled.

"Hell yes!" She laughed.

Just then, a door creaked.

"Did you hear that?" Jen asked nervously.

They looked around and noticed the lights were on in the house.

"Lets get our clothes and hide out in the pool house." Austin jumped out of the water, then bent down to lift Jen out with one easy swoop.

They were frantically gathering their clothes when the pool lights came on. Jen panicked for a second, until Austin grabbed her hand, assuring her with a smile. They ran towards the pool house, giggling along the way.

"I guess we woke the house up." Austin chuckled.

Jen blushed, thankful it was dark enough that he probably couldn't tell.

Once safe in the pool house, Austin sat down on the sofa and motioned for Jen to come snuggle in his arms.

"So how was that for your first time skinny-dipping?" he asked.

Jen rested her head on his shoulder, smiling. "New, but definitely an experience," she replied.

"I hope it was a good one." Jen could hear he was smiling.

"Definitely an experience I'll never forget," she replied, and sank into the sofa with him in post-coital bliss.

VESSEL

BY MISSY MARTINEZ

My eyes open. I'm blinded by a light so white, so pure it's heavenly. Suddenly, I'm being raised up. A hospital bed. A white and sterile room. There are three men and two women huddled around a clipboard. I can't feel my body, but I am calm. Looking down, I can see I'm in a hospital gown.

What happened?

Two burly men hulk through the door wheeling a dolly. Time to go. I'm taken down a series of dizzying corridors until the blinding light of being outside embraces my body. I'm loaded into a large truck, and the metal door slams with a deafening clang.

Darkness.

I don't know how much time has passed. The door opens and I am wheeled out by the two men. Quickly, I try to scan my surroundings.

A high rise building.

Chandeliers.

Doormen.

I'm pushed into the elevator and we ride straight to the top.

Penthouse. A well-dressed man greets us the second the elevator doors open. I try to look at his face, but I'm only able to focus on his mouth. I can't look at his eyes, nose, body.

Mouth.

As I stare, he signs some papers and I am his.

He wheels me into his loft. Wall to wall concrete. It's cold. Lifting me off of the dolly, he then sits me on a soft, cigar-brown, calf-leather couch. I still cannot move.

Then I feel his soft hands on the small of my neck. Hands that have never touched dirt. He sweeps my jet-black hair to the side, and *click*. I hear something like buttons being pressed; he's typing something. He's typing something on me. Electricity runs through my body and with each jolt, I feel more alive.

I can move my head.

I look down at my body. Two large, heaving breasts rise and fall with every breath I take. When he approaches me, I look up at him—again, I stop at his mouth and devote all my focus and energy to it. It opens.

"I'm your master. Do you understand me?"

I nod and an unexpected smile comes over my face. This is why I'm here.

"You are here to please me. Nothing else. You are a toy and I will treat you as such. Do you understand?"

An even bigger smile spreads across my face. I open my mouth to speak, but nothing comes out. I am a vessel.

A container.

A hole.

He grabs me by the hand and my body follows. He leads me through his dwelling. More of a compound than it is a home. I like the coldness. We enter a large room and he points to a bed.

"Go," he commands.

Without the slightest hesitation, I obey and sit on the large, soft bed. His taste in decor is impeccable. Money has shaped him into the perfect man. He stands in front of me and unbuttons his dress shirt. The starch in it is so fresh it almost sounds like crisp construction paper as it's unbuttoned and dropped to the ground. I reach my hands out to drag down his chest and I notice for the first time my nails are manicured red. He is warm.

I am not.

He forcefully grabs my hands, which startles me, but instills no fear.

"Did I say you could touch me yet?" he says sternly.

I am overwhelmed with shame. I must please and obey him. He disrobes me. My itchy hospital gown feels like razors against my smooth and poreless skin.

I am finally free.

He caresses my body. His hands are as soft as silk, yet restrain so much power and destruction in them. He gathers my hair into a makeshift leash and pushes me down to my knees.

I'm instructed to unzip his pants. I oblige. I can see a large bulge fighting against the fabric of his slacks—it's obvious which is winning. Delicately, I pull the metal zipper down and am immediately greeted by his large member bursting through the open fly. I am in awe. His cock is perfect in every way. I open my mouth and look up at him and stare at his mouth. I'm awaiting to hear my orders.

"Be a good girl, and suck," he authoritatively coos.

I am a mindless pleasure machine here to service his exquisite dick. I restrain myself from devouring his member like a ravenous animal. I have self-control.

I nuzzle my face against his throbbing shaft, letting his smooth skin caress my face. Delicately, I take him into my hand, as if it were paper and his cock were a sword. Ever so slightly, I graze my lips against his glistening tip. I apply his precum like lip gloss. I gaze up and stare at his mouth while slowing dragging my tongue across my lips, savoring his sweetness.

He says nothing, but he smiles. I have pleased my master for the first time.

Grabbing my hair, he turns me into a steering mechanism. He drags me across the spacious master suite to a chaise. My knees scrape against the cold concrete floor and it excites me. My nipples become sharp points that I worry will cut my master. He leans back onto the chaise, the leather groaning as he settles in. He snaps his fingers and a spark shoots through my naked body. I crawl to his side.

"Begin," he commands.

I open my mouth and slide his even harder cock in. My mouth instantly floods his shaft with hot saliva, bathing his dick in what I understand from his expression is pure ecstasy. Dragging my smooth tongue up and down his never-ending cock, I feel my mouth muscles begin to tire, but I don't let that stop me. I am a machine. I pull my mouth away from him, long spit strands spread between us like a dew-covered spiderweb. The spit rope breaks and my breasts become striped like a tiger. I apologize for making a mess and soiling his property and request punishment. He cradles my chin with the delicacy of holding a baby chick. A gust of wind hits my face before the pain. His hand slaps me like the smoothest brick. Another spark shoots through my body. I am excited.

"Thank you, master," I pant.

I am a dog in heat. Without warning, he plunges his throbbing cock to the back of my throat. I feel a shock in between my legs that I have never experienced before. I want more. I start sucking with the force of a black hole. He never once breaks the rhythm his sword makes as he slides it down my throat with the precision of an award-winning marksman. My eyes are watering with tears of happiness. Tears of pride in being able to please my owner. Tears of needing war.

He pulls himself away and I want to sob like a child who

dropped her ice cream cone. He walks to the kitchen. I meet him there by slinking on the floor, like a lioness stalking her prey. I sit on my knees at attention, eager for him to speak to me again. He reaches into a small refrigerator and pulls out a bottle. I can't make out the label, but I would never question my master's taste. He rummages through a drawer and pulls out a corkscrew. I ask myself why he hasn't grabbed glasses. He pops the cork, and I don't flinch. He starts pouring golden liquid down the drain.

The kitchen is filled with the aroma of sweet, bubbly yeast. He snaps his fingers and points to the bedroom again. I crawl across his freezing floor; every knee-drag is agony and ecstasy that could never exist without the other. He walks slowly behind me as I slowly make the trek across the arctic tundra that is this concrete hallway. I feel his eyes examine me.

Critique me.

Covet me.

He has a plan for my body. I am meat. He instructs me to lie on the bed, legs spread. Grabbing the empty bottle, he puts it to my mouth, and instructs me to suck it. I take the cold glass into the inferno that is my mouth. I suck the vessel with the same passion and bravado as my master's cock. He pulls it away before placing it in my hand.

"You know what to do," he says encouragingly.

I feel another surge race through my body. He is right, I know what to do. I lift my long legs up with the limberness of a gymnast and spread them wide, like a good girl. I grip the bottle with both hands and slowly slide the neck of the bottle into my sweet slit. The chilled glass extinguishes the fire inside me. A flood of juice surrounds the bottle. My back arches and my toes point. I am in heaven.

I can see Master standing at the edge of the bed. His mouth has the faintest trace of a smirk. I'm his good girl. As I slide the phallus in and out of myself with the fervor and cadence of a locomotive, I am on the verge of exploding.

"Stop!" he commands. "You can't cum yet."

He pulls the bottle away from my rigor-stricken hands. He puts the glass neck to his nose and breathes in deeply. He closes his eyes and smiles. Master stands over me, and I have to divide my attention between staring at his mouth and his still rock hard erection. He pushes my closing legs wide open again, kneeling before me at the edge of the bed. I feel the softest sensation in the universe graze my sweet spot. His tongue begins to slowly massage my clit, causing me to grip the sheets as if they were the only thing keeping me from floating away. There are lightning bolts of sweet electricity shooting in between my shaking legs. I focus on his mouth as he makes love to me with his tongue. His hot breath, his cool saliva, his muscular tongue—he is perfect.

He quickens his tempo and intensity. I feel that sensation of explosion again. My legs tremble, my back arches, my heart races, and I am flooded with intense waves of vibration crashing and rolling up and down my body. I have seen the face of God, and he just ate my pussy. Master brings himself to my face. I can smell my sweet juices on him.

"Clean me," he orders.

I drag my tongue across his lips and around his reddened mouth. I taste like honey.

He shoves his hand in my mouth as I finish cleaning myself off of his face. He slides his long, slender fingers down my throat. My mouth is overflowing with spit. He pulls out his hand and rubs the waterfall of saliva over his steel cock.

"On your hands and knees," he orders.

I flip over and assume the position with choreographed excellence. My back instinctively arches as I present my round, smooth ass to him. I am in heat. He drags his cool fingertips down the curves of my backside. He spreads the dripping lips between my legs and I am filled with the ultimate sensation of fullness. My tight cunt stretches to accommodate the titanic thickness of his member. I feel as if I'm being impaled by pure happiness. I open my eyes, shocked that such pleasure could actually exist, and am greeted by the sight of his mouth agape. Even my wise and all-knowing master wasn't prepared for the joy I am capable of providing him. He slides his cock all the way out of my pulsating fuck-hole. That is all it is. A warm, tight refuge for his saint of a shaft.

I exist solely to make him come.

I am nothing but a whore.

Once he pulls his cock out of me, I see his perfect dick glistening with my juices. I am filled with longing. I don't want him inside me; I need him inside me. He rubs his engorged tip on my pulsating clit, massaging my most sensitive parts with his. I rock my hips back and forth, trying to entice him into penetrating me once again. Master reaches his arm up towards my neck, constricting my slender neck with intense pressure. The second he applies force, he plunges his prick deep inside me. I am flooded with the most exquisite sensation ever to grace the face of this earth. He keeps his hand firmly fixed around my neck as I writhe in rhythmic cadence with each of his strokes. He releases me from his hand control and I gasp for air as I am overwhelmed with euphoria and what feels like hundreds of mental orgasms.

I breathe in large gulps of air. He truly is my master.

"Good girl," he commends.

He has to fight my grip to pull out of me. When he succeeds, I've never felt such abandonment and disappointment. His cock completes me. It is my purpose. My prime directive.

Master grabs me by my hair, and I instinctively arch my back to the point I feel my spine snap in half like a twig. I feel a hot, fiery sensation engulf my arched ass, as if I've been branded like prized cattle. His hand has marked me as his property. My badge of honor. Something wet drips down my sacred area.

"Are you ready to be a good girl?" he asks, knowing the answer full well.

I spread my ass.

Finally, he enters my other fuck-hole. My asshole is his now. I'm astonished he can even fit his gargantuan sword inside this sacred and holy ground. I moan and groan as he slowly eases himself into my virgin ass. He romances my asshole with the precision of a professional ballroom dancer. My cunt overflows with sweet syrup. I am engulfed in the rapture of pure delight and immense pride with every stroke that he rewards me with, and I am amazed that I am able to accommodate him in such a small, tight space.

This is what I am designed for.

He picks up the pace of ramming my virgin bottom, each stroke fulfilling my destiny of being the perfect fuck doll. He deprives me of his cock once again, but quickly returns it by tossing me onto my back, which is relieved to have a break from arching so intensely. He shoves his member into my pouting mouth. My taste buds are engulfed with the flavors of my most intimate crevices. My delectable asshole juice mixed with my intoxicatingly sweet vagina nectar, all topped off with the exquisite delight of the precum dribbling from his pulsating rod. After I sufficiently savor every drop of the sweetest dessert ever concocted, he surprises my senses by entering my jealous cunt. He cuts off my air supply once more as he fills my love cavity with every inch of his meat. His cock impales me, like Vlad during wartime in the 15th century. I can't hold back my climax any longer. Master has been bringing me to the edge of pleasure for forty-five minutes. He grinds his hips into me with every powerful stroke.

It's as if he, too, is a steam-powered machine designed for fucking.

Master finishes me off with a flurry of strokes that are a blur, like a racecar in its final lap. I scream as small explosions of pleasure detonate between my legs and resonate throughout my entire body. He lets out a moan like a lion roaring on the African plain. The rush of his hot cum inside me fills me like a cup of hot tea. It spills out of my still-contracting slit; I am overflowing with his reward. He orders me to clean up the mess for which I am responsible. I reach my trembling hand down between my legs and am greeted by a waterfall of jizz. It sticks to my hand as I bring it to my mouth. The flavor is indescribable. This is what heaven tastes like. I am enthralled and enveloped in a warm feeling of pride and satisfaction of knowing I did my job.

Like a good girl.

He collapses next to me, chest heaving as if he just ran a marathon. "You are a good girl," he coos as if he just won a battle. "Best investment I have ever made."

He takes me by the hand and guides me to his bathroom. We both enter his slate stone shower. The glass fogs as he washes my body with lavender-scented soap. I am glowing with pride for completing such an honorable task. This is his way of rewarding me. He towels me off with a fabric. Maybe angora. I feel born again. He dresses me in my robe; I am repackaged. He walks me back over to the metal stretcher.

He kisses my forehead, "Thank you, good girl."

I memorize all the lines of his mouth. I love him. I feel his warm hand on the back of my neck.

Click, *click* of the buttons as he presses them.

Then, blackness.

NIGHT MOVES

BY RACHAEL MADORI

"Evening, Miss Audrey."

The doorman had the door held open for me before I even put my car in park. I texted Michael on my way over to make sure she wasn't home. I hadn't seen him in almost a week, which wasn't normal. He never questioned it, though—he was only there when I came for my dose of him.

Tonight was different.

When I got to his door I knocked loudly. He came to the door with his same sense of calmness.

"Good." He smiled. "I've been a little"—he scanned my body—"frustrated tonight." He waved for me to enter.

Instantly high at his insinuation, I snapped myself out of it to stay focused. I gripped my choker and walked in. "I actually need to tell you something." I looked up at him. Every motion I made, every look he gave me, I filed away in my memory, aware that this was quite possibly the last time I'd be near him again.

"Oh?" He closed the door behind me. "What's that?"

"I did it." I was nervous. "I got what I needed. I can leave."

He wasn't expecting that news. I saw a shift in his eyes, but it dissipated quickly. *What was that?*

"Well, look at you." He walked closer to me and twirled a lock of my hair in his fingers. "I almost forgot we even had a deal." He smirked and looked at me a way I hadn't seen before I tried to shake it off discreetly. "I think it's best you leave the city immediately."

His words stung, but he was right. No doubt I had made enemies, and I didn't have that plan for nothing. "I was thinking the same thing . . . " I trailed off, unaware of where this conversation would bring us. I was trying to buy more time near him before I had to kick my habit.

"However." He dropped the lock of hair that was between his fingers and stared me fiercely in the eyes. "I would hate if you drove all the way here for nothing." He was playing our conversation cool but I couldn't help notice a difference in his demeanor. I stared back at him with unsure eyes and then he walked away, disappearing down the hall for a minute.

I waited for an order.

The streetlights looked like fractals through heavy tears welling up in my eyes. That didn't help my driving. I sped down a lonely highway, running from a situation I had put myself in again. All the windows were down. My dark hair whirled around and stung my face. There was something about the wind blowing violently through my car that made it feel like I could be swept away into the sky, never to be seen again.

I liked that.

The road was slick from a heavy shower earlier that night, and my headlights illuminated the path. Every bright green exit sign beckoned me, but nothing would stop me from getting what I wanted.

Fuck! I pounded the steering wheel with the palm of my hand.

What a fucking mess. I caught a mouthful of my hair as I shouted, only the wind hearing my complaints. The night hadn't panned out the way it was supposed to. I was supposed to find my way out, but I saw my golden ticket slip away as quickly as it had come. I was angry. And there was only one place I went when I was angry.

The thing about my life is that it had always been out of control. And sometimes, a girl needs control. That's what led me to be speeding over the bridge to that side of town. My day-to-day was utter chaos. There was only one constant; this one thing made living a little more bearable, as fucked up as we both were. Butterflies fluttered in my gut with every mile inched closer.

I pulled up in front of the apartment building I knew all too well—one of those floor-to-ceiling window high-rises. Unlike my personal hole in the wall back over the bridge, it towered over my small frame. I threw my car in park and leaned back for a second to take a deep breath. Toying with the black choker fastened tightly around my neck, I stared up at the skyscrapers, now realizing the sun was beginning to creep through the night. I had lost track of time. I hopped out and headed towards the door, not even bothering to wipe my tears or save face when I stormed past the doorman.

"Evening, Miss Audrey." He nodded like he always did while holding the door open for me.

All I could think about was what awaited me. Whatever it was. Whatever tonight had in store, as long as I got to feel my anger dissipate by drinking the tonic that was his presence, didn't matter. It wasn't my nature to make a single thing, a single person, such an integral part of my life, but he was different.

With most of the people I dealt with, it was drugs, adrenaline, or money.

Well, this was my fix.

Everyone has a fix, whether they admit it or not. No one wants to confront the one thing that proves we are all, in fact, weak. I came to terms with it years ago when this all started. I learned from a young age that everyone has a dirty little secret. I learned we all roll around in the dirt with it until we're good and damn well ready to give it up.

I was not ready yet.

The butterflies in my stomach had now turned into bats, and my heart raced as the elevator climbed up. Seventeen . . . Eighteen . . . Nineteen . . . Top floor.

I was already at his door before the elevator closed shut and began its descent back downstairs. *What's going to happen when it's time to end this? Have you fallen too deep into the rabbit hole?* Every time I found myself here, I had the same thoughts—and this time was no different. It didn't matter, though; the thoughts never deterred me. It wasn't like I wanted to be anywhere else in the world than standing right here with my knuckle against his door.

I hope he's here.

Knock, knock.

I hope she's not.

Some time passed, I'm not sure how much. I waited. I always waited. What could I say? I was addicted.

I heard the clicking of locks, and then he opened the door, somehow still looking handsome at God-knows-what hour. Sometimes I couldn't believe he was a real human being. Adjusting his black robe, he didn't seem fazed to see me standing there absolutely disheveled—like this was just another Tuesday night for him. Tilting his head, his dark eyes rolled over me slowly. He held my gaze for what seemed like an eternity.

"Come in." He moved to the side, motioning for me to enter. "It's late."

I dipped into his apartment and threw my purse on the dining room table. I turned around and looked at him. I knew he could see the desperation in my eyes. His arms were crossed, face expressionless.

"What did you get yourself into this time, Audrey?" He moved towards me, reigniting the violent butterflies. He brought his body an inch from mine. My skin instantly heated up from his vicinity. My mind raced.

Finally.

He ran his fingers along my waist and glided behind me. Placing both hands on my shoulders, he leaned forward to whisper in my ear. "You always run here to escape." His breath sent shivers down my whole body. "You're always running." He chuckled, lips still lingering at my ear. I closed my eyes and let his pure existence wash over me.

Without warning, he gripped my throat from behind and wrapped my torso in his other arm, grabbing both my breasts. He pulled me so tightly against him it startled me.

"I needed you," I gasped.

I imagined a dark smile spreading across his face. He ran off lust, like he was some kind of machine, fondling me, nuzzling my hair and taking a deep breath through his nose. His breath on my skin made my pussy ache. He pressed his mouth to my neck. "I know you only come here when you've been bad." He loved having the upper hand. "Have you been bad?" He nipped my ear just enough for the sting to heat me up even more.

"Y-Yes." I loved the way he made me shake. The way I felt like a ridiculous little girl. There wasn't a rule on Earth that I obeyed unless he was in the room. It felt good. So good. "It was just another job, b-but it all went wrong," I stammered as his hand glided down my stomach and beneath my pants.

He played with my panties for a moment and then slid past them.

"Mmhmm . . . Mmhmm . . . " He nodded as he listened to my

explanation. I squirmed. The chill of his fingertips resting on my clit made me lose focus. He bit my ear again.

Shaking, I tried to continue my point. "There was a new guy there, one I'd never met before. He was a rat, Michael. He fucked it all up. I ran. I-I had to. I don't know what happened to our crew but I got the hell out of there."

My nefarious night life came as no surprise to him.

"S-So . . . I ran here. To you." I dropped my head, knowing full well how much he savored proof of my obsession.

He whirled me around and pushed me against the wall. He grabbed my neck forcefully this time and turned my cheek towards him, inspecting my lack of resistance for whatever he chose to do with me. "You can lay with me tonight, but you won't be rewarded for waking me up at this hour." He pressed his lips hard against mine. "As much as I would love to take out some frustrations on you." He moaned into my mouth then pulled back quickly and walked off. "Get undressed." He threw his hand up as he walked into his bedroom and waved for me to follow. "I'm tired."

I couldn't say I was in love, as much as I could say I was addicted to that man. I knew he wasn't mine. I knew he didn't love me. Michael wasn't the kind of man to give me emotion. That wasn't what I needed. He gave me something else. He tapped into something I didn't know existed. Somehow he dug past my wild spirit and found a secret desire to be controlled. A desire of mine that was hidden in the deepest, darkest corners of my mind. Places I was too frightened to go. The obsession wasn't healthy, and I knew it. But that didn't mean I wouldn't have given my left leg for just one more night next to him.

Tomorrow morning when I awoke, he would be gone. I never asked where he went; I already knew. He would be with her, with the woman in his life who was there long before I came into the picture. The one who didn't let him explore the darkness he so desperately needed to unleash on me. I didn't ask questions—I grew tired of that after the jealously wore off. You can only be jealous of someone for having something you want. I didn't want Michael the way she had him.

I wanted him exactly the way I had him. In the dark of the night, when I needed parts of me explored that I feared to do so myself.

As expected, I woke up alone. I rolled over and reached for my cell phone, my tired eyes and smeared makeup making it hard to focus on the time. I rubbed my eyes and waited for them to adjust to the bright screen.

Holy shit, it's late.

I threw the covers off and stumbled around the room, picking up my clothes and getting dressed. After quickly splashing cold water on my face, I took a moment to look in the mirror. I stared at the black choker I never took off. Michael bought it for me. He said I always had to wear it, and of course I obeyed. Five years now, he'd been my fix, and I had yet to understand how he infected my mind. I looked at myself in the bathroom mirror; I was a mess. I tried to give myself a pep talk. I had bigger things to worry about right now.

Remember the goal.

I stared myself down in the mirror. *You don't want to be stuck in this fucking city forever.*

It was always back to business when he wasn't around, when he wasn't hypnotizing me. Last night was a major loss. My gaze shifted downwards to the running water. I tried, but couldn't stop the tears. *You were so close!* I punched the counter. Blood dripped from my knuckle. *Shit.* I winced at the pain radiating through my hand. I splashed more water on my face, grabbed my purse, and ran out the door.

"Afternoon, Miss Audrey." The doorman nodded as I headed out.

Once I got to my car, I noticed a parking ticket tucked neatly under my windshield wiper. I grabbed it and slumped behind the wheel. *Goddamn it.* I tossed the bright yellow paper into my purse and sped off. There was no traffic heading back over the bridge, which was nice, but at this hour, in this direction, it was to be expected. Not many people headed to that side of the city, and for good reason. Although I had lived there my whole life, I held no loyalty to those streets. I hated them just as much as I hated the life of crime they forced me into. I wasn't as stupid as some of my counterparts, though. I saved every bit of money I could, from whatever jobs we pulled here and there. That was the goal—Get. The. Hell. Out.

Remember the goal.

I sighed my mantra as I rolled down the windows, letting the wind in. All I wanted was to escape that place. Ever since I was a little girl, I fantasized of walking out onto a balcony somewhere and being met by a warm beach breeze. Palm trees swayed in my mind while I dreamed of peace, quiet, and a new slate. I lost myself along my drive daydreaming.

Remember the goal.

I was jolted back to reality when I pulled in front of my excuse for a home and was met by Tyler. He was there last night, and he ran up to my car as soon he saw me pull up.

"Audrey, Jesus Christ! I'm glad you're okay." He leaned through my open window.

"What happened? I bailed as soon as things went south." I ran both hands through my hair, sighing. "Are you okay?" He knew I asked because he had the money on him before shit hit the fan. He knew I knew. I was in business mode; I never had time for games. Leaning against the steering wheel, I looked up at Tyler sternly and waited for an explanation.

"Hey, h-hey, I know what you're thinking. Look, Josh and I got out of there together and bailed to his cousin's house for a few hours," he stammered. I made him nervous. "Our cuts are safe. At least us three got lucky. I'm not sure what happened to the others, but that's why I've been waiting outside your place all day."

Standing outside my place looking like a shady idiot, was more like it.

"I don't want any bad blood between us. You know I got you." Tyler slid his hand into his hoodie and pulled out a thick envelope. He dropped it quickly into the car and I shoved it in my purse.

I smiled up at him. "Damn, we actually caught a break for once." I'd known him the longest out of everyone with whom we did business, but it wasn't like I really trusted anyone. "I appreciate you looking out. You have no idea how much I needed it."

He smiled and shrugged. "You know I always got your back, Audrey."

His words stung. Not because I cared much at all for him, but because I knew how he felt about me. Tyler had no idea of my plans to skip town once I saved up enough money. Personally, I think he was stuck in this delusion that we'd fall in love one day and enjoy a life of crime together, a real modern-day Bonnie and Clyde.

Ridiculous.

I snatched my purse and got out of the car, making sure to lock it behind me. I gave Tyler a nod as I headed up the steps to my place. "I'll see you around. I got some shit to take care of."

He shot me a quick smile and headed down the street. I shimmied through the broken front door to my building. Once I got into my apartment, I instantly hit the locks, plopping onto the mattress on the floor before taking the envelope out of my purse. I held it to my chest. Closing my eyes, I finally exhaled a huge sigh of relief. Every envelope brought me closer to escape. I jumped up and headed to the bathroom. Running my fingers along the sides of the mirror, I wiggled it off the wall the way I had so many times before. Behind it was the black duffel bag where I held all my dreams. I counted what Tyler had given me, then tossed it in the bag and quickly replaced the mirror. I headed back to the mattress in a daze.

Holy shit. I fell to my stomach on the bed and rested my face in my hands. *You fucking did it.* Tears began to pour. I had been working nonstop in that hell with my head down for five straight years. I did, and had done to me, unspeakable things. Finally, I had enough to escape. Enough to run away forever. I hadn't felt high like that since . . .

Well, since Michael.

Shit. Michael. I was always so focused on the end game that I never thought about what would happen when our deal was over. When I was ready to disappear. We would feed each other's needs until the time came. I never thought about when it would actually come. I knew I only needed him to numb the pain from my everyday life, but I wouldn't need that where I was going. I had to run this last bit and never have to run again. I wasn't too prideful to admit that I was afraid to live a life without him.

Remember the goal.

I sat on the money for a few days while I got things in order. Packing my life up in that little car, I tried to figure out when to talk to Michael. The idea of cutting ties with him made me nauseated and cold. *Can I trust myself on my own? Is disappearing really going to save me?* It was such uncharted territory, my head spun. I recalled what it felt like to be in his presence, to feel his touch. My body ached. I closed my eyes and thought of his smell and his stern eyes. Drunk off his memory, I lay on the bed and caressed my body. My pussy was looking for any and every recollection of him. I lost myself in my mind for a while when a single thought violently shot me back to reality.

What if the next time is the last time?

I jumped up and looked out the window at the stars. Quickly I headed out the door, and drove off.

* * *

"Come."

He beckoned me sternly. I walked into his room as he lay on the bed, the moonlight hitting his solid body in an image of absolute perfection. My pussy dripped at the sight. "Undress. Come lay." He threw his hands behind his head as he waited for me to join him.

I slid onto the sheets and cuddled against his warm body. He wrapped his arms around me and held me for a moment. There was power but a new sense of intimacy behind his actions. It made me unsure and excited.

"Is this our last night together?" I whispered, my head on his chest as I stared off into the darkness.

"Yes." He held me and closed his eyes. "It is." The words made me hold onto the moment even tighter. I didn't know what to think.

I nestled into Michael's chest. I felt powerful being cradled by his strong body. It was as if we had both let our guards down for a moment. It felt like we were just two bodies waiting to see what the darkness of night had in store for us.

No plan. No deal. Just us.

He slowly ran his fingernails across my bare back. The sensation made my nipples perk up. I felt my heart rate increase just a touch. There was nothing left to the imagination with our naked bodies lying intertwined. My sense of uncertainty dissipated and was replaced with sexual ache. I sat up and let Michael nuzzle my neck, his sleepy yawn giving me shivers.

My yearning increased and he took to it slowly, creeping his lips down my neck. It seemed the saltiness of my skin left him thirsty for more. He moved his mouth down my body, kissing my collarbone gently and grazing me with his teeth. I was trying to hold back, but let out a gasp, squirming in an attempt to hide my goosebumps. Michael always loved it when I squirmed. He danced his fingertips from my knee up to my inner thigh, not giving me the satisfaction I was burning for yet. He ran his fingers lightly over my pussy lips, through the wisps of my bush, and up my belly.

"Mm," I moaned softly through my heavy breaths. I felt a deep twinge from my pussy. I couldn't deny the heat. I could tell Michael was aware of what he was doing to every nerve in my body when I saw a smirk on his face.

He moved up my belly and outlined the curves of my breasts, pausing in anticipation at my nipples. Back and forth, he caressed beneath each breast. Finally he gave me a bit of relief by drawing circles around my nipples then giving them a soft pinch. I sighed. He cupped my breasts and kneaded them gently. I could tell the frustration welled up in him just as much as it welled up in me. He leaned close and sighed into my ear like he was starving. Michael grabbed me tightly and pulled me close, trying to hold back from pouncing.

He ran his hand back down between my thighs. I tightened my legs playfully and didn't allow him entry. I could only hold out for a second. He slid his fingers up and down through my lips; I was already moist from his toying. The tips of his fingers were wet now and he moved up to my clit, pinching it.

"Oh god," I panted. His touch was unlike anything else. The pain and pleasure of being played with drove my body insane. His fingers lingered at my hole while he pressed my clit with more force. He drew his teeth and nibbled my neck. I started to groan louder when he quickened his pace on my clit. I could barely think through the pleasure. *Please don't stop. Please don't stop.* Without any warning, he jammed his fingers inside.

I gasped in surprise and searched for him in the darkness. I couldn't be without his taste. We locked lips and he quickened the rhythm of his fingers, sliding in and out as I pushed myself into his hand.

"Yes . . . Y-Yes!" My orgasm building inside me as he pumped my pussy faster and faster. "Don't stop!" At that, he slid down the bed and threw my legs over his shoulders, opening me up for him to devour. Fingers still slick with my juices, he furiously pushed them in and out while pressing his mouth on to my clit. I couldn't help but let out a scream of ecstasy. My orgasm washed over me like a wave of fire. I tightened my legs around his head but that only made him suck harder. My body writhed against his face as I basked in every vibration of my climax. I sank into the sheets and watched Michael lick up my juices.

"Come here," I croaked, and grabbed him. I glided my hand down his solid stomach to search for what I wanted. I quickly found it throbbing in my palm. Our tongues danced in manic ecstasy while I stroked him. I could feel all the blood rushing to his cock and without hesitation, I guided him inside me. We both let out a groan the second he filled my soaking cunt. We ground our hips together, and every inch of his shaft hit me.

My juices spilled out with every thrust and another orgasm burned within my core. Michael pulled me in closely, his five o'clock shadow grazing my upper lip. He moved faster and faster, harder and harder until he began to convulse inside me. I could feel the cum right on the edge of bursting out of his cock. We were drunk off each other. He pounded my sopping wet pussy and gripped my body as if it were his very own life force.

"O-Oh my god," he growled. His animalistic moans of pleasure awoke something hot and primal inside of me. His body shuddered, about to explode.

"Cum inside me!" I wailed as I wrapped both my legs around his waist and clawed his back. "I want to be filled with you," I begged into his ear, about to unleash my own orgasm that I had held onto for too long. My words sent Michael over the edge and my cunt clenched around him. Tears welled in my eyes as he pushed deeper into me than ever before.

"Yes!" His cock unloaded, his cum hitting the back of my pussy and filling me to the brim. The sensation threw me into a final wave of euphoria that swept over my entire body. My pussy contracted violently with his cock still inside me and I screamed as all my juices saturated us both.

Out of breath, we both collapsed with my legs still around him. He kissed me passionately as we shook from sensitivity. We had soaked the sheets. Reality steadily came back when Michael slid out and keeled over next to me on the bed. I nestled into his chest.

We lay there in silence for a while, trying to catch our breath and figure out what would happen next.

"I will only admit this once," he said, "but a selfish part of me was hoping you would never reach your goal."

It pissed me off that he was so selfish, but I had mostly learned to take his faults in stride, the way he took mine. We were nothing if not honest with each other.

We were both fucked up.

"Me too," I admitted shamelessly. Nothing else was spoken between us. I rolled over and let him pull the silk sheets over our bodies. The coolness of them was comforting. I could only assume from the silence that he drifted off to sleep quickly.

I closed my eyes as a smile rolled across my face, despite knowing this was the last time I would be in that dark moonlit room ever again. There was no point in soiling the moment by wracking my brain with thoughts of the future. Tonight, I'd let myself be carried off into a peaceful sleep.

The next morning, for the first time, I awoke before Michael. I slid out of bed without waking him and got my things together quickly. As I unfastened the choker around my neck and placed it on his nightstand, I took one last look at him sleeping there.

Remember the goal.

I shut the bedroom door behind me and headed out of the apartment.

"Good morning, Miss Audrey," the doorman said, flashing me a smile as he held the door open.

I breathed a huge sigh of relief while on the road that morning when I bypassed the bridge and took an exit that led out of the city. My mind wandered while my hand hung out the window and flew through the wind. Michael would wake up soon and find me gone. He wouldn't ask where I went, because he already knew.

I would be where I always wanted to be, long before he came into the picture.

THE MISSING INGREDIENT

BY ABELLA DANGER

"I can't believe this is happening. Is this a dream?" he asked as he entered me.

It was the first time anyone had ever fucked me, taking my innocence. I moaned in a low voice as he thrust in and out, in and out of my virgin hole.

I felt pressure, I felt full; I felt something, but not the feeling that I had imagined. Not the feeling that I had learned to give myself with my finger, or by humping my pillow.

This was . . . different.

He turned me over, gripped my butt cheeks, and thrust in and out. Groaning louder than me, he kept a constant rhythm. I was close, but not quite there, when he pulled out, ripped the condom off, and released his milky load all over my butt.

That's it? I wondered. I was underwhelmed, but I reminded myself I had made him do this. In fact, I had begged him.

You see, somehow I was the only virgin among my friends, the only one left silent during conversations of sex with "the loves of our lives" and "the ones." Of course, I knew the first person I had sex with wouldn't be the love of my life or the one, and I didn't want him to be. I didn't want to deal with the headache of a high school romance just to have an excuse to experience sex.

I wanted to lose my virginity to someone I trusted, someone I could never hate. Who better than my best friend Evan?

I spent almost every single day with him, and that day was no different. We were in our friend Greg's room: Evan, me, Greg. Three friends hanging out, no big deal. But suddenly, something came over me—I can't really explain what. Maybe it was the way Evan looked that day. Maybe it was where I was in my cycle. Or maybe I was just finally ready to do the damn thing.

I looked right at Evan. "I want you to take my virginity right now," I told him, plain as day, in front of Greg, who did nothing to hide his shock.

"Please don't ask any questions, just please do this for me, I'll never regret losing it to you," I continued.

"Sure," Evan replied as Greg watched on in awe.

So there I was, the deed was done, I was no longer pure and innocent. Just disappointed. Why hadn't I felt the way I had with my finger, why wasn't it like grinding on my pillow?

I had to know.

When I woke up the next morning, I felt a burning sensation concentrated in my thighs. *Great*, I thought. I was finally "a woman" and the only difference was this awful soreness. All day I felt the discomfort—in school, up and down the countless stairs; at dance, marking as many movements as I could; in the parking lot standing beside my friends and their cars. This was always my favorite part of the day—not that we did much, but when you're young and constantly told what to do, doing absolutely nothing is the best.

"It was so fucking tight, Andy," said Evan, recounting details to our friend about our little affair. I stood there with a grin as

I watched a similar one form on Andy's face, listening to Evan's account of the deflowering.

"When is it my turn?" Andy joked, laughing.

I smiled. "Okay," I casually replied, to everyone's surprise.

The thing is, Andy, Evan, none of them understood how badly I wanted to cum from sex. How much I wanted to experience the orgasms I gave myself with a man during sex, like the way girls gushed over and over all over a dick in a porno.

I craved that.

Andy didn't have his own car, so we went inside Evan's, all three of us in the back seat of the Cadillac Escalade. I turned to face the window on Evan's side, arched my back, and stuck out my plump ass cheeks that separated just enough to show the opening of my tight little pussy. With surprising force, Andy entered me—in and out, in and out.

I felt full again.

Just a couple minutes into the hard pounding, Evan unzipped his pants and gestured my mouth towards his cock. Without any thinking necessary, I opened wide as drool fell onto his dick. I swallowed it whole, gagging, gargling, and sucking as I got fucked harder and harder. As if they had done this kind of thing before and they were seasoned pros—or had seen it in a porno. They turned me around and I was now facing Andy's cock. He entered my mouth as Evan entered my pussy, and I heard myself moan.

They're using my holes as they please, I thought, and smiled. I was starting feel full, I was starting to feel good—but still, not the way I made myself feel.

Once again, the boys came, and I was left unsatisfied.

We jumped out of the humid car that now smelled distinctly of sex, latex, and weed. The boys high-fived each other and let me know this was going to happen again. It was odd, but even though I wasn't getting the pleasure I wanted from them, the fact that they were so pleased from our encounter gave me a certain amount of satisfaction. After our little impromptu threesome, we went to eat greasy burgers and then I went home.

Smelling like sex, latex, and weed, I took off my school uniform, my dance leotard underneath, then finally my underwear and stepped into the shower. I turned the water as hot as I could ever possibly bear, stroked my hair down to my chest, and gripped onto my boobs. My hands ended at my clit. I loved feeling the difference in the wetness between the water, my pussy juice, and spit, the way they're all wet in different ways. I rubbed my clit with my back leaned against the wall, clenching and relaxing my ass cheeks in a steady motion, muffling my moans. I didn't stop until I came so hard I almost fell in the shower. I turned off the water, dried myself off, and lay on my bed.

Why can't I feel this way during sex?

In the next few months, I went on to explore sex with even more boys—eight more to be exact. I loved having sex because I loved how much guys enjoyed having sex with me. I felt full, felt good, felt something—but not feeling *it. It,* as in, the sensation I craved so much to enjoy with someone, caused by someone, a man.

Six or seven months after losing my virginity, I was sitting at home wondering what to do with my day when I got a text from my friend Evelyn.

Evelyn: *I need your help*

Me: *What's wrong?*

Evelyn: *I'm on a date with this guy and he doesn't want his friend Kim to be alone, can you keep her company? ;)*

Me: *Sure lets meet by the Ferris wheel*

Evelyn: *thank you I love you!*

As I made my way towards the bright and colorful ride crowded with teenagers around my age, I laughed at how eagerly they were all waiting to have a couple minutes of private makeout time.

"Hey, baby girl!" I kissed Evelyn on the cheek in proper Miami greeting fashion. "What's up?"

"Jane, this is Michael, and this is Kim." Evelyn introduced us, and my eyes met Michael's big, round brown eyes decorated by shapely yet thick eyebrows. I'd never felt such an immediate, intense, uncontrollable connection. Although in reality it only lasted a few seconds, our gaze felt like hours.

I decided then that the boy would be mine.

"Hi," we said at almost at the same time, while simultaneously kissing each other on the cheek. I could feel the lips between my legs get moist in the corner of my thighs.

"We want to go on the Ferris wheel," Evelyn continued, oblivious to the insane connection Michael and I had just made.

"Sure, I'm down," I answered, and we walked up to the line. In an unbelievable stroke of luck, the conductor stopped us, informing us that Michael and I couldn't bring our food on the ride— my candy apple, his large soda freeze.

"Well, we could just wait while you guys go," I spit out. "I just got this and I don't wanna throw it away."

"Yeah, it's so fucking hot I need my drink," Michael agreed, and my heart skipped a beat.

Still oblivious, Evelyn shrugged."Ok, meet us at the green monster rollercoaster!" she yelled, as she led Kim to accompany her in the line.

Michael and I walked away and found a bench in between the two rides. We talked and talked, completely ignoring our phones for once. Michael was in college. A man. He was experienced, but not overwhelmingly so, and he had things to teach me.

I had things I wanted to learn from him.

Finally, our faces got so close to each other's it was almost a test of who would kiss whom first. He grabbed my face with his strong, yet delicate, hands and kissed me so hard I could feel it in my fingers, in my toes, my hair. And in between my legs.

I melted. I had never been kissed like that. It was barely an open-mouthed kiss, but it had so much passion behind it.

That night in bed, the next morning in school, the afternoon during dance, all I could think about was Michael—his eyes, and his mouth, his voice. I wanted him so bad that I was scared to have sex with him, frightened he wouldn't like it, fearful of rejection. I briefly thought of Evelyn, but decided she would understand, and went back to fantasizing sex with Michael.

Right when I got home from school, he texted.

Michael: *Can I pick you up?*

Me: *yes, please*

I came outside dressed in my favorite low-rise jeans and a cropped tank top. Suddenly shy, I looked to the ground until I opened the car door and my eyes met his again.

"Hi," we said to each other, again almost at the same time. I got in and closed the door. He again grabbed my face with those strong, delicate hands and kissed me. If it were possible, this kiss was longer, more passionate, had more tongue, and then . . . he stopped. I smiled, he smiled, and we drove away.

By the time we entered his bedroom, I was so nervous that my hands were sweating. My clit was tingling, and I wanted him inside me. He placed me on his bed facing him, and I couldn't even speak.

"I know you're nervous," he said, "but I promise, I just want to make you feel good."

Shocked, I wondered silently to myself, *Is that really what he wants? To make* me *feel good?* I didn't know whether to believe him or not, but the fact that he even said those words were enough to have me gushing downstairs, so I let him go on. He opened his mouth while grabbing my neck.

"Give me your tongue," he commanded, and so I did. Sucking on it gently, but with emotion, he then kissed my chin, down to my neck, back up to my ears, down my shoulders to my chest, then my stomach, and, only then, finally, did he place his mouth is on my lips—the wet aching lips between my legs. I had never had anyone ever do that to me—he made out with my clit softly, sucking and humming. Running his hands all over my body, I clenched and relaxed my ass cheeks in a rhythmic motion with my eyes closed, moaning as loudly as I ever had, gripping onto the headboard for dear life until I felt this sweet, oh so very sweet, orgasm just burst. It wasn't the feeling I knew so well how to give myself. It was better. And he wasn't even finished. Breathing heavily, I couldn't believe that had just happened.

He kissed me, and I could taste my cum. I loved it. I loved that he made me cum. I told him so.

"Can I do it again?" he asked, and I nodded with a shy smirk. Picking me up in one swoop, he put me up against the wall—my cheek, my chest, my stomach. He grabbed my hair with one hand, placing the other on the small of my back, and forced me to arch it until my face was right under his. Euphoria. His hard dick slid inside me and I, to my disbelief, I came again after just three strokes.

"You're so good, you make me feel so good," I yelled as he thrusted in and out, in and out.

"This is all for you," he whispered, "this is all to make you feel good." The walls of my vagina clenched as I came again. This time, he came too.

We went to his bed. I couldn't stop smiling. I finally had an orgasm with someone, and it was exactly how I didn't want to lose my virginity: in a high school romance I knew would never last past my teen years. But I guess that's what the missing secret ingredient was all along.

I think it was worth it.

ON THE PROWL

BY ANNIE CRUZ

Frankie had a rule: Never fuck someone more than once. Unless they were good. Then she fucked them twice. If she fucked them more than twice, they gained potential to be booty calls. But she got bored easily, and it was very rare for her to have a repeat offender.

On Friday, Frankie ended the week with an impromptu threesome with her roommate Andrew, and his friend Brandon. The thing about Frankie was this: when she saw something she liked, she went after it. She and Andrew already had a history together because they used to bang regularly, back when they were just neighbors in downtown LA. Even after Andrew found himself a girlfriend, they remained friends, and eventually, they moved in together. They had only been living together two weeks when Brandon and a few girls came over to hang out. Frankie had never met Brandon before, but was drawn to him immediately and knew at some point before the end of the night, he would be inside her. So naturally, it wasn't long before she was locking lips with him on the couch.

As the place cleared out towards the end of the evening, Frankie led Andrew and Brandon back into her bedroom. No one wasted any time as clothes went flying all over the room, and two cocks were immediately shoved down Frankie's hungry throat. Both were rock hard and ready for all of her holes. Brandon lay on his back as she lowered her wet cunt on top of his long dick. Andrew came in from behind, sliding his thick cock into her asshole. They swapped positions throughout the night, double-penetrating her and making her cum continuously until the sun came up. Brandon soon shot his load all over Frankie's mouth, while Andrew finished all over her ass.

Sound asleep after getting properly fucked by two men, Frankie woke up to Brandon underneath the covers, his mouth inhaling her pussy. To her right was Andrew, whose hard dick was now in her hand as she slowly stroked him.

"Fuck," she said under her breath. "I'm gonna fucking come."

Andrew's hand quickly moved to her throat, choking her just the way she liked. "Cum for us," he whispered in her ear.

As Frankie's body moved uncontrollably on the bed, Brandon's hard cock was already inside her tight, wet, coming pussy. Andrew silenced her moans with his cock, while Brandon fucked her until he unloaded a second time all over her pussy. Flipping her onto her knees, Andrew quickly thrust his dick into her from behind for his turn. As she felt her cunt tighten around his dick, he knew she was going to cum again. He quickly flipped her over back again, pulling out and shooting a hot load down her throat.

Just another Saturday morning.

Later that evening, Frankie went on the prowl. While partying with friends at a local nightclub, she eyeballed two good-looking guys by the bar. As she walked past one of them, she grabbed his ass like a perverted man would do to an unsuspecting woman. Walking past, she turned to catch his stare. He smiled. She joined them and exchanged numbers. Two nights later, she would fuck one of them. This was how Frankie operated: One down, onto the next.

On Sunday there was Wes, whom she'd met online, and upon meeting in person, he'd instructed her to answer the door in nothing but a sweater and high heels. She did what she was told, and he rewarded her with his tongue up her ass. That same night, she met up with Joseph, who was completely unaware that he was feasting on Wes's sloppy seconds.

Those were the first and last times she would see either of them.

On Tuesday there was Michael. And on Wednesday, there was Patrick.

Patrick was a beautiful creature. His photos on his dating profile did him absolutely no justice. There was sophistication about him. He was well dressed, stood tall, had light brown hair, hypnotizing green eyes, and a tight, fit body. Frankie was in such lust the second she let him in the front door. In his hand he held a bottle of champagne, which they immediately popped open before going straight for the bedroom.

Smiling, Patrick shut the door behind him just before grabbing Frankie by her face and sinking his lips into hers. Pushing him onto her bed, she straddled him—their tongues colliding as they continued to kiss. She slowly started to grind against the raging hard-on growing in his pants. With their lips still locked, she gradually found her way onto her knees, staring up at him as she unbuckled his belt. It was the moment of truth, and she felt like she won the lottery. Not only was this guy good-looking, but the monstrosity she had just unleashed from his pants was thick and beautiful. She wrapped her lips around the head of his dick and slowly took him, inch by inch, down her throat. Tears slowly trickled down her cheeks as she choked on it for a moment, and as she gasped for air on the way up, Patrick pulled her onto the bed.

"Sit on my face," he said.

Frankie did what she was told. He ate her cunt from underneath her, while she sucked on his dick at the same time. After a few minutes of this, she spun around to face him. Teasing him, she slowly started rubbing her wet pussy against his cock. He quickly grabbed her by her hips, stopping her then lifting her so that her cunt sat just above his dick. A soft moan escaped her lips as she lowered herself onto his big cock.

He pulled her close as her ass bounced up and down to the rhythm of her riding him. Releasing herself from his embrace, she sat upright, grinding her hips back and forth against his dick, feeling his head hit that sweet spot inside her cunt. Her pussy got wetter and wetter as she was close to climaxing.

"Oh my God," she said quietly.

Her body convulsed and shook on top of his with such intensity. For a split second, she couldn't remember the last time she'd had an orgasm that powerful before. Patrick didn't seem to think twice before swiftly flipping her over, so that he could be on top now. With her legs spread wide, she gave herself completely to him, feeling him fill her up with every inch of his gorgeous cock. Thrusting deep inside her now, he grabbed her throat, choking her as he fucked her. Her cunt tightened as she was about to cum again, and when he pulled out, she squirted all over the both of them at the same time his dick exploded all over her stomach.

In their post-orgasmic bliss, they lay next to each other for a few minutes. Patrick started dressing himself as Frankie lay lifeless in her bed, completely cum-drunk and dick-high from whatever dickmatizing trance he had just put her into. There had only been two other men in the history of Frankie's sex life that had the power to dickmatize her with their incredible skills.

Patrick was the third.

The following morning, Frankie woke horny and wet. Opening her bedside sex drawer, she grabbed her magical vibrating wand.

Its firepower blew any tongue out of the water and could get her off clitorally in a matter of seconds. Thinking about the amazing sex from the night before, she closed her eyes and turned her toy on to max speed. She thought about the way he smelled and the way his cock felt inside her pussy. She thought about the way he choked her and what it would feel like if he fucked her in the ass. She thought about the way they both came at the same time, the look on his face, and how hot it was. Grabbing the sheets, she screamed loud as she came.

Later that afternoon, Patrick contacted her.

"Ready for round two?"

"I've been ready. I played with myself this morning thinking about last night," she confessed.

"I've got to say," he continued, "choking you out and making you squirt really got me going. I want to be rougher with you."

By that evening, he was back again. Round Two. In her bedroom, they made out like high school kids just before he threw her down onto her bed. He climbed on top of her, shoving his cock down her throat, face-fucking her and eating her pussy at the same time. Tears started running down her face as she choked on his cock. He moved his way to the edge of her bed, pulling her into him as she kneeled on all fours before him. Gripping her hips, he slid his dick nice and slow into her tight, wet pussy. He flipped her over onto her back and grabbed her throat as he looked deep into her eyes with his thick cock inside her. As he choked her, her pussy contracting as she was about to cum. Pulling out, she squirted all over herself and his chest. Her pussy was even wetter now, and he slid his dick back into her. Pounding her tiny cunt, he began choking her even harder.

"Harder," she could barely speak as he gripped her throat.

He fucked her harder, and her pussy exploded with more squirt, spraying him in the face. She could tell he was getting turned on the more she did it. Flipping her over onto her knees, he fucked her from behind. Licking her fingers one by one, she inserted them into her ass, while he fucked her pussy. Staring at her, each finger disappeared into her ass. Frankie shoved her fingers down her own throat, producing even more spit, and rubbed it all over her ass. All she could think about was earlier that morning, playing with herself and fantasizing about what he would feel like in her ass. Her entire fist was up her ass now, making her pussy extra tight on his cock.

Patrick was teasing her butt now, rubbing the head of his dick against her asshole just before Frankie grabbed it completely and shoved it in for him. This was what she was dreaming of. As she felt the head break the seal, she backed herself onto it, while she was still on all fours. He fucked her in the ass for a while until he fucked her cunt again. She was on her back again when he filled her pussy up. He grabbed her throat gently at first, then his squeeze gradually got tighter and tighter. Suddenly both hands were on her throat, choking her.

"I'm gonna cum," Frankie gasped as he plowed his cock into her.

He pulled his cock out, coming all over her, and at the same time, she squirted everywhere.

Two days back to back with the same lover. Unusual. But that would be the last time she would see him for a while.

The following few weeks were busy. There was Josh, Mikey, Cody, Alex, Nick, Jordan, Matt, Anthony, Trent, Sebastian, Ben, Jeff, Ross, Robert, and James. There were also the occasional ladies like Monique, Dani, Chanel, Rita, and Nikki. Nikki was a lesbian visiting LA from NYC who Frankie had picked up at a popular gay bar in West Hollywood. She pulled Nikki back to her place, where she dominated her into submission. Frankie licked, fingered, and strap-on-fucked Nikki into a coma.

Thanks for blowing my mind in bed, she had texted the morning after.

One hot afternoon, Frankie sat across one of her many conquests in a Hollywood coffeeshop. Jeff was a manly man, standing six-foot-three with dark brown hair and a beard to match his husky, built stature. Like a sexy Paul Bunyan, he was the spitting image you'd find on vintage covers of the Hunky Lumberjack. He was a trainer at her gym and deemed untouchable by everyone because he was engaged.

Untouchable? Challenge accepted.

Sex was just sex to her, after all.

As they chatted over cold brews, Frankie plotted how she would lure him back to her place, which just happened to be down the street. She was determined to unlock the mystery in his pants when her phone went off. It was Patrick. It had been a few weeks since she last heard from him. She felt it, from the moment she saw his name pop up on her phone; she was still captivated by his sex.

Jeff caught her smiling as she stared at her phone. "Good news?" he asked curiously.

It was decided then that she would put her conquest with Jeff on hold. As soon as they parted ways, she continued her conversation with Patrick.

Patrick: *My twin brother is in town visiting for a couple of days. We are going to come fuck you up. I want to give him you as a treat, while he's in town. Will you be our toy?*

She was completely unaware that Patrick had a twin brother. This excited her as she had never been with twins before.

Frankie: *Ok!*

Patrick: *Do you have any ropes to restrain your arms? We want to put you in complete submission and destroy you. Also, put on a hot outfit for us.*

Per his request, Frankie threw on a black bikini top on with a tight waist-cincher and short skirt with no panties. Black patent knee-high goth booths with buckles running along the sides matched the leather collar she had received as a gift from someone at her favorite BDSM shop. She answered the door in a long trench coat, hiding what was underneath. The ring from the collar poked out slightly, and as the twins entered her front door, Patrick yanked on it.

"Good girl," he said, obviously pleased that she had followed directions accordingly.

Christian followed him inside. He was precisely identical to his brother. Frankie was seeing double, and this turned her on even more. Why it had taken her so long to scratch this feat off her "fuck-it" list was beyond her.

Frankie dropped the trench coat to the floor, revealing her outfit. Patrick disappeared, leaving her alone with his twin. Despite having met barely five minutes prior, Christian didn't waste any time. He grabbed her, pulling her close to him, and caressed her slowly from her lips to her collar down her chest until his hands met her pussy. He tossed her onto her bed, ordering her to display her ass for him. With her face buried into her sheets, she did what she was told, waving her firm butt in the air for him.

Frankie was unaware of what was to come next. Christian startled her as he dove face-first into her ass and cunt. Like his twin, he was a giver. She licked her lips as his tongue glided slowly up the slit of her pussy to her perfect asshole. After Christian tongue-fucked her holes, Frankie didn't want to waste any more time. She spun around to face his cock, which was identical to Patrick's in every way. Wrapping her lips around it reminded her of the last two times she'd had Patrick's in her mouth. Christian grabbed her by the back of the head and slowly started fucking her throat. As she gagged and cried, Patrick returned to join them.

Like a well-directed porn film, Christian quickly moved onto the bed on his back, while Patrick readied himself for the next position, pushing Frankie on top of his twin. They were in such sync with each other; it was as though they had done this many times before. She climbed on top of Christian, sliding his hard cock into her tight little cunt as she faced him. Without hesitation, Patrick moved in, shoving his dick into the same hole that his brother was currently inside. Squealing, Frankie jumped.

"It's too small," she said in agony. "My pussy. It'll never fit the both of you."

"Sorry," the twins said in unison.

"It's okay," Frankie said breathing heavily. "Just do it here instead."

Recovering from the double-stuffed pussy surprise, she licked her fingers just before shoving them one by one into her ass with Christian still snug in her cunt. As her fingers worked their way up her ass, he began thrusting upward, filling her up slowly, while his twin worked his dick into her ass with her fingers still inside. A ferocious moan filled the room as the twins worked their cocks inside her holes.

"Yes, fuck me!" she screamed as they double-penetrated her. She came hard, pulling her fingers out of her ass to grip the sheets right above Christian's head. He pushed her gently off his dick, and moved it towards her butthole. The twins were now cock-to-cock in her hungry ass.

They moved rhythmically as they shared the same hole, slowly fucking her, feeling her, and feeding into the way her body responded to their every move. She was moving on top now, backing her ass onto both their cocks, fucking them and controlling the depths at which their dicks moved inside her. They sat still for a moment as she did this, grabbing her ass and her hips. In their triangular embrace, Christian's lips found hers, and they kissed. Patrick spanked her a few times just before her fingers found its way back in her ass again. She was triple-stuffed when she came again.

The triangle finally broke. Patrick moved on top, fucking Frankie in her cunt again. He plowed his dick into her for a few thrusts before pulling out and blasting his hot load onto her face. Christian began pulling her by her hair, forcing her to crawl on her hands and knees towards the edge of the bed. With her face painted in his twin brother's cum, he shoved his cock in her mouth. She sucked the cum straight out, feeling it shoot down her throat. After he finished, Christian left her motionless on her bed. Frankie was high again, unsure of what had just happened—not only had she fucked identical twins, but they double-penetrated her asshole.

She worked her way from the bed to the bathroom, and walked in on the twins sharing her shower. This was clearly not the first time they had done anything like this before, and she wondered what else they might be into.

As she got dressed, Frankie realized how much she liked variety (she could make an exception for twins). Everyone smelled different, tasted different, looked different. That was her favorite part. New partners meant new experiences, and this was something she craved. Frankie had lovers from different countries who were all young and old, male and female. Nothing seemed to satisfy her completely, and she loved that.

After the twins walked out her front door and bid her goodbye, a sexy Australian messaged her.

Frankie: *Come over.*

And he did.

TALES FROM CANCUN

BY LOTUS LAIN

Carla was everything her parents wanted her to be—intelligent, healthy, active, obedient, wholesome. Her whole young life, she had striven to fulfill the idea of a Squeaky Clean Teen Dream. She studied hard and received excellent grades. She was passionate about her participation in the student union, and her volunteer work feeding and clothing the town's homeless. She was the kind of girl who would kindly reprimand her friends for smoking weed during the school week or drinking alcohol at weekend parties. And, of course, during her senior year of high school, three of the better universities in her home state of Arizona tried to lure her with scholarship offers. She did as her parents encouraged, and she never veered off course.

Danielle, her best friend, was much more popular than Carla. She was an outspoken cheerleader and volleyball player. Carla admired Danielle's athletically crafted physique, which was likewise admired by the boys. She dated any football or basketball player she wanted, from their high school or any other. Not as smart or gifted as Carla, but at that age, among their peers, that was hardly as important as Danielle's perky butt in volleyball shorts.

Leading up to the last week of high school, the buzz of senior trip was in the air. Loads of seniors from all four local high schools were planning on making an epic journey to the sparkling beaches of Cancun, Mexico. But Danielle had some disappointing news for Carla. When her parents had made her choose between her senior trip and a new car, Danielle chose . . . the new car.

At first, Carla was upset, panicked even. *How will I have a good time in Mexico without my best friend?* Of the two girls, Danielle was far more comfortable making friends and snagging guys for them to make out with.

The solitude of Carla's vacation journey set in immediately. Neither her mother nor her father was able to drive her to the airport because of their work schedules, so she took an airport bus by herself and, once she got to the airport, watched as other high school seniors escorted onto the airplane by crying mothers and fathers—some even bearing bouquets of flowers for the send-off.

Oh c'mon, she thought. *Really?*

But once she was settled in her seat on the plane, her solitude began to dissipate, replaced by the excitement of a full week in Cancun as the others senior trippers yelled over seats, high-fived each other, took snapshots with disposable cameras, and frenetically buzzed about the adventures they were going to have, what with the legal drinking age in Mexico being eighteen. They one upped each other, anticipating how drunk they would get, which clubs they'd be partying at, and how many times they would get laid.

En route to the airport, Carla tried to distract herself from the disappointment of not having Danielle with her by pondering things like the snorkeling in Cancun and its Mayan tourist sites, but here, in the midst of this excitement, a new leaf turned within her. A new sense of self. She was emboldened and empowered by her independence. Sure, she had the company of a couple hundred other graduating seniors from her hometown, but she didn't really know them, having never hung out with them. She could leave her academic and overly responsible self in Arizona and let loose, indulging the part of herself she had never let surface for fear of being judged.

Carla wasn't a virgin, but one partner didn't exactly classify her as a slut. But something within her wanted to let all that pretense go.

Fuck it, she thought.

As the plane descended on the shining city of Cancun, the teenagers on board cheered raucously and, ignoring the "fasten seat belt" sign, triggered their belts and jumped up in excitement. Carla, staying put in her window seat, stiffened when a cute, buff, milk-chocolate guy squeezed in next to her to look out the window.

"Hey," she said, noticing his deep dimples and big white smile.

"You ready for a wild week in Cancun, baby?" he said. As Carla opened her mouth to answer, he continued, "I'm Patrick." He stuck out his hand.

"Paddy, check it out!" yelled someone a few rows back.

"But all my friends call me Paddy," he said, rolling his eyes. "I'm from Cali." He sounded like he was boasting. "And you are?"

Guys like this from her hometown wouldn't normally give her this kind of attention, so Carla was a little surprised by how friendly he was.

"A-A-Arizona," she said. Patrick chuckled. She smiled bashfully. "I mean, I'm from Arizona. My name is Carla."

"Well, nice to meet you, Carla the Cutie," Patrick said, shaking her hand. "Hopefully we can party together soon!" And with that, he jumped over to the next row of seats to high-five some of his friends as they congratulated each other on making it there. Carla settled back into her seat, basking silently in the excitement of her peers going nuts around her.

The plane emptied out into a rudimentary-looking airport, which resembled something like a Greyhound bus station. The swarm of teens piled into rows of parked shuttle buses that would take them to their hotels.

As Carla boarded her bus, it didn't take her long to notice that this wasn't a Greyhound. Bottles of Corona were being popped open and passed down the aisles to all receptive hands—the beer provided by the bus drivers themselves. Carla stowed her luggage overhead and, as she sat down, hesitatingly stuck out her open hand and intercepted a frosty Corona. She stared at it like she was examining one of the Mayan relics she hoped to spy on a history tour. She chuckled at the thought, raised the bottle to no one in particular, and, after a trepid sip, happily guzzled down the rest on the road to the resorts of Cancun.

Because Danielle had left her hanging on this supposedly most epic vacation of their lives, Carla was plopped in a room with two other girls from a neighboring high school that had an extra bed. But upon their first interaction, Carla could tell these girls were much like Danielle—party girls. They brought multiple bikinis, where Carla had merely brought a single one-piece bathing suit. They unpacked thong panties and daisy duke shorts, as Carla unpacked cartoon-character-logo boy-style panties and Bermuda shorts. Carla hadn't quite realized how childish and prudish she came across until she saw their tube tops and spaghetti-strap tank tops compared to her wide-strapped, full-backed tank tops.

Geez Louise, do I need to loosen up, she thought. Luckily for her, Becca and Erica were helpful new roomies who offered to share some of their more suitable clothing for clubbing and partying in a Mexican paradise. Nervously outfitted in a tube top and some daisy dukes, Carla embarked on her first night out in Cancun, with Becca and Erica leading the way.

Their first stop was Señor Frog's, the premier destination spot for American tourists in Mexico. As they entered, "The Thong Song" by Sisqo was playing loudly over the speakers. Carla's eyes widened as she saw a row of varying butts, out of their shorts and skirts, on display on the main stage.

"Show us your goods, ladies!" shouted a Mexican bartender into a megaphone. "Best thong gets free shots for an hour!"

Screaming and madness filled the bar, and everyone was smiling, laughing, and getting absolutely shit-faced. Not wanting to be left behind, Carla decided to take two shots with her roommates, before losing them in the crowd. Pushing her way through the sea of sweaty coeds, she found herself in the front row of onlookers, staring up at the all the butts, the club lights glistening, highlighting the wave of pleasant posteriors gyrating above the crowd. She saw guys slapping some of the nice butts, and secretly wanted to participate. They were so soft and bouncy and welcoming. She had always been attracted to girls, but had no way to express it in her conservative hometown. *What the hell?* she thought, feeling the effects of two shots, and started smacking butts as well.

Suddenly, a random guy close to the stage tapped Carla's arm and motioned for her to come up. "Get up there, girl!" he yelled, vigorously beckoning her. "Get your ass up there!"

The guy started pulling her up to the stairs before Carla could even react. She got up on stage and squeezed in among the fifteen or so other chicks already on stage, thongs out, asses in the air. Carla forgot that she wasn't wearing a thong, but her full-bottomed, boy-style panties instead. A warm wave of embarrassment washed over her as the fact suddenly dawned on her. Feeling stupid, she looked to her right to see the guy that brought her up on stage motioning wildly for her to drop trou.

Fuck it! she thought, not only pulling down her shorts, but her juvenile panties, mooning the whole crowd. As wild and liberating as it was for Carla, most of the drunken revelers didn't even notice the difference between her full ass cheeks out and the girls next to her with thongs up their cracks. She reveled in the thrill of simultaneously getting her butt rubbed by the crowd and rubbing other girls' butts while she was up there.

A cute chick with short blonde-streaked brown hair won the Thong Contest, and she was paraded around the stage holding an oversized cup of alcohol with Mardi Gras-style beads coming out of it. *Ew, gross*, Carla drunkenly thought of the beads and liquor in the same cup. Then she spotted Patrick—Paddy—sitting at a table with guy friends. He did a double-take and immediately jumped up to greet her.

"Hey cutie," he said. "Funny seeing you here." He wrapped an arm around her shoulder. Carla could tell he was just as buzzed as she was.

Liquid courage came over her as she blurted out, "You're so cute yourself. Wanna make out or something?"

Carla's awkwardly direct approach made Paddy laugh. They walked outside as he motioned something to his boys about being right back. Suddenly, he stopped and turned to Carla, aggressively pressing his face up against hers to make out with her. He had big, full lips and warm arms and shoulders. His tank top allowed Carla to feel on his muscles as they kissed, while his hands started making their way down to her daisy dukes. As the kissing grew more passionate, he began to unbutton them.

Carla pulled away to get air and they made eye contact as he slipped his hand, palm side up, into the front of her panties. He touched her pussy lips, his middle and index fingers sliding around the edge of her before slowly making their way up and in. Carla gasped a little. They continued kissing and the more she let go, the more she enjoyed his fingers inside her. But when Patrick started unbuttoning the fly of his cargo shorts, Carla pulled away, immediately turned off.

"Where are you going?" he confusedly exclaimed.

"I . . . uh . . . I just . . . I just can't do this out here," Carla said as she made her way back to the main street, leaving Paddy with his dick in hand. Clearly confused, he yelled something incoherent from the dock zone as he fidgeted to get his shorts zipped up. Carla looked back one last time before venturing to find her hotel roommates.

Their next preplanned Mexican group adventure was a boat ride to Isla Mujeres—Women Island. There would be more drinking contests, more teens from all over America, and more opportunities for debauchery.

As soon as they docked, the teens scrambled to a giant stage set-up where an emcee was already giving party commands to drink and flash boobs for those Mardi Gras-style beads. Carla, once again, quickly became separated from Becca and Erica—who were really only looking out for each other—leaving her alone in a sea of strangers. She decided to get drunk as soon as possible and let the liquor lead the way.

Pin-balling from body to body, Carla found herself face to face with a short, spiky-haired young guy who immediately began making out with her. *Blink-182*, she thought to herself, and, before she knew it, he was leading her by the hand to a bathroom stall.

The gel in his spiked black hair was starting to melt in the heat of the night and she instinctively started using toilet paper covers to wipe him down so he wouldn't sweat on her. This time, though, she was undeterred, and it seemed suddenly they were having sex, right there in the bathroom stall on the Isla Mujeres. She panicked for a second and looked down, relieved to see a condom on him as his hard dick went in and out of her

Relief turned to excitement as she continued bouncing on his cock. He was surprisingly strong for his frame, holding her up and bouncing her with each thrust.

Suddenly, a worker from the small island popped his head over the stall they were in. He laughed maniacally, saying something Carla couldn't understand *en español.* The two teens, surprised, broke away from each other, buttoned up, and went back outside where the party was raging. But they were still drunk and hornier than ever, so without thinking, they urgently searched for a more clandestine sex spot, stumbling upon a dingy boat pulled way up on shore. It looked like a decoration prop for the party happening close by, it was pulled so far up shore. And to Carla's drunken eyes, with all sorts of campy nets and buoy stuff, it seemed fake enough to have real sex in.

"Look, it's not a real boat," she blurted, yanking his arm. "We can do it in there!" Just as suddenly, she stopped and whipped around to her newfound fuck-buddy, looking him squarely in the eye. "Wait, what's your name, even?"

"Oh, now you wanna know?" He laughed before noticing that she was serious. "Jacob Taylor," he said, trying to affect some seriousness as he stuck out his hand.

"Hi," she said, shaking his hand with drunken vigor. "And, uh . . . " She searched for an obvious question; there had to be one. "Where are you from?"

He looked at her questioningly and chuckled. "San D," he said, then waited a beat to see if that was all. She averted her eyes to the upper left searching for more, when Jacob Taylor from San D grabbed her by her waist and began making out with her again.

What's with meeting cocky guys from California? she wondered. As the making out turned back into full on fucking, that same worker again popped up again to spoil their private party, interrupting with that same ridiculous laughter. This time, though, Carla could make out some words—something about needing to hurry up and get back to the main area because everyone was loading the main boat to go back to Cancun!

Thank you, three years of AP Spanish, she thought as she and Jacob Taylor jumped up out of the boat, which Carla maintained was a fake, and ran back as quickly as they could to the boat headed back to Cancun.

The final two days of their debauched Mexican vacation was approaching. Carla headed out one evening to get food and wander around. Bored, she decided to drink two giant margaritas and a tequila shot at what had become her favorite little coffee shop and was immediately buzzed.

Letting the liquor lead the way, she walked around until she came across a giant super club that was trying to resemble a rave. There were go-go dancers painting on people's bodies with glow-in-the-dark paint. There were whistles being blown to the beat of the music, there were guys doing light shows with neon lit-up accessories. It was strange, but in keeping with her carefree attitude, she walked right in and joined in the fun.

Carla was unsure of how much time she spent there, but she did come out with a giant glow-in-the-dark sun painted on her back and to the realization that it was now nighttime. Many more people were out, making it much easier to get lost in the crowd.

Carla boarded a tourist taxi bus and was approached by two men that sat on either side of her. They were Mexican locals, she could tell, and they were talking to her in Spanish. Emboldened by liquid courage, Carla enthusiastically engaged in a broken, drunken Spanish conversation with them. As they laughed, the men moved closer, putting their arms around her, suggestively grazing her arms and legs. The other American teens on the bus looked at Carla with concern. One girl called out to her, "Are you okay? Do you want to be with them?"

"Yeah," Carla responded, waving them off. "I'm fine." But

even she didn't believe herself when she heard how blurred her words sounded coming out.

Despite her better judgment, Carla exited the tourist taxi bus with the two men and as they walked, they started playing with her hair, kissing her neck, letting their hands explore. Carla's earlier enthusiasm had morphed into serious discomfort when all of a sudden, a tall, muscular man with dark curly hair and a baseball cap scooped her up from the ground and threw her over his shoulder. From the mount of his shoulder she saw him push the two local men down by their foreheads. "Get outta here!" he bellowed loudly as the two men scattered. "You don't wanna go with them, sweetheart," he said to Carla over his shoulder. "They were taking you to the real Cancun. The Cancun that tourists don't come back from."

His words sent a chill down Carla's spine as she recalled the early warnings they'd all received about staying in the Zona Hotelera, or Hotel Zone of Cancun and never going into the real city.

"O-okay," she managed. "Th-thank you." *How will I pay this handsome stranger back for rescuing me from certain rape*, she thought, *or . . . death?*

They ended up at his hotel overlooking the beautiful sparkling lagoon of Cancun. He looked like a bro version of Superman, all tall, muscular, and strapping. The encounter and subsequent thoughts of what might've happened if her hero hadn't come along had killed Carla's buzz. But as he continued giving Carla safety tips, she was becoming enamored. Carla kept asking him his name, which was John or Jack or something she swore started with a J. John, or Jack, was good humored about it.

What's in a name, she thought, chuckling. John, or Jack, chuckled with her, having no idea what it was she was laughing at, but being sexy nonetheless. One thing was certain—he was like no other man she had ever known. High school boys were wimps; they had no balls. They certainly wouldn't endeavor to rescue her like that.

She could tell John or Jack was a grown man—especially with his huge body on top of hers. She kept feeling his broad shoulders and hairy chest. He pumped away almost as if she wasn't there. And as he thrust his impressively large cock into her, she looked over the details of his body almost as if he wasn't there, either. It was the most disconnected sex Carla had ever experienced—not that she had much to which she could compare it. Nevertheless, she wasn't sure who either of them were having sex with, because it wasn't each other.

After showering and getting redressed, she let her hero walk her down to the lobby as he hailed the tourist taxi bus. She waved goodbye to him and though it seemed logical to return to her hotel room and go to sleep, she was feeling invigorated and awake; ready for more action.

Back in club Dady'O, Carla could get drunk to the sight of acrobatic dancers spinning on poles hanging from the ceiling in outfits lit up by blacklight. She also had the urge to snag another vacation hookup before week's end tomorrow.

Sure enough, just as she put her drink down, she noticed a handsome man in a suit checking her out. Letting the liquor lead the way, Carla feigned confidence, cocking her head back in the unspoken beckoning motion to "come hither." His brownish blonde hair, chiseled jawline, and perfect set of bright white teeth fully presented themselves as he approached.

Carla spoke first. "My name's Carla. I'm from Cali," she lied.

"Great," he said, smiling bigger. "I'm James. I'm from New York . . . the city." Looking around the room, he changed course. "What's with all the kids? Are you with them?" He tugged on her colored wristband, which all the teenage revelers were given at the start of the week to get into clubs and bars. It was a dead giveaway, as she noticed he didn't have a wristband, but rather, cufflinks.

"Yeah," Carla conceded. "I'm with them. We're all here for our senior trip. We just graduated. But we're not all here together.

Some people are from other schools and other states." She hated the way that whole sentence sounded childish to this man in a suit. But he still seemed interested, so she played it cool.

"Well," he shrugged. "Like I said, I'm from New York and me and a couple of business buddies decided to come down for the weekend to let off some steam. Nice to meet you, Carla from California. So where in Cali are you from exactly?" He casually motioned to the cocktail waitress for two more drinks, then turned back to Carla.

All she could think of was Snoop Dogg and Dr. Dre saying "Westside" all the time, so she said, "I'm from, uh, the Westside . . . of LA," feigning that California confidence she had mocked earlier in the week.

"West LA, huh?" he said. "That's cool. Wanna dance?" He held out his hand for her. Carla accepted and soon, a little grooving and shimmying turned to freaking it, right next to their table. He pulled his pelvis up close to Carla's backside. She could feel his bulge hardening as she bumped and ground her butt and hips into him. She was wearing a short dress and could feel his thick hands sliding up her thighs as they gyrated in unison to the beat of the music.

She hadn't realized that she had forgotten her panties at Superman John or Jack's hotel room, until James from New York—the city—slipped his hand up to her uncovered pussy lips. "Ohhh!"

He looked at her, impressed as if she had gone sans panty on purpose. She blushed, shrugged, and coyly smiled, like she was saying, *Yeah, I did.*

From there, the making out became heavy, as did the finger-banging. Everything was a blur around them. Everything felt good: the music, the dancing, the buzz, making out with this super handsome businessman. James. From New York.

The city.

Before she knew it, the two had made their way to his hotel room. James was aggressive, but respectful. He was tall and slim—not very muscular, but still defined. He would take little moments to slow down and caress Carla's body—legs, breasts, and hips—all while looking her in the eyes. He put his head between her legs and ate out the pussy that had been fucked earlier by Superman John or Jack.

Carla wasn't in the habit of shaving her whole area down there. She'd shave just the lips, so she could see James from New York enjoying his meal beyond a small mound of curly hair as she looked down at him. He came up and kissed her, saying, "Now taste your own slutty pussy!"

She had never kissed a boy right after he had eaten her out, with her own juices still on his mouth. It was nasty . . . and exciting. *Warm lemon cake*, she thought to herself.

He got on top of her and planted his cock right in her face. Carla's upper body was trapped beneath his legs as he lowered his massive cock onto her mouth. She felt the tip of it touch her still-closed lips. As her lips parted, she could feel the precum on his tip, so she licked it up. She licked the head of his dick with slow, long, fat-tongued strokes that stretched down the length of his shaft. James tilted her head back and plunged his cock down into the back of her throat. He brought her head up to his cock with one hand and continued finger-banging her with the other. Carla was under his command. She sucked and sucked his big cock, gasping for air at times, but he would not relent, plopping his throbbing cock right back into her slobbering mouth.

After Carla's pussy tightened up and came on his fingers, James dove in deep with his now-raging hard cock. She gasped and felt a chill as he slid his thickness in through her pussy lips. The rippled veins showing, his engorged penis filled up her wet pussy walls. James was powerful and strong, and he pumped and plowed his cock into her missionary-style, then turned her sideways.

"Get on your knees doggie-style, bitch!" he said.

Normally, Carla would be offended by being called a bitch. But he was fucking her so good and deep just like she'd always wanted, so she allowed the "bitch" bomb to fly and took her deep-down, doggie-style dickings for as many more pumps as he had.

She was lost in ecstasy and getting close to cumming. With each pounding thrust, her round ass bounced against his pelvis and his balls slapped up against her clit. He spanked her ass and she yelped in surprise. He spanked it again from the other side as his pumping cock thrusts became faster and more vigorous. "Cum for me, bitch! Cum for me, you little slut!" he demanded.

Carla let out a resounding, "Oh, my God!" as an overwhelmingly powerful orgasm took command of her whole body, making her pussy clench up tight around James from New York's cock, making him cum as well. She shook as she came down from the magnitude of such an intense fuck.

She fell to the bed, and James fell down next to her. They lay there panting, recovering from what had just gone down. James pulled off the condom with a loud snap and tossed it into a nearby trash can. Carla got up and went pee, then stood in the bathroom doorway, watching James looking out the window of the hotel room.

"So?" she said.

"So that was probably the best sex of my life!" James exclaimed, turning to face her with a giant grin that made Carla light up with delight. She skipped over to him and gave him a hug.

"That was like no other sex I've ever had," she told him, looking up into his eyes.

"My friends are not even gonna believe me," he said. "None of them have ever been with a black girl before."

"Well, none of my friends are gonna believe I hooked up with some business dude from New York. James from New York—the city," Carla added, smiling.

They both looked at each other almost as if trying to figure out how they'd gotten there.

"Well, I don't mind writing you a note," Carla proclaimed, grabbing the hotel issue pen and pad.

"Okay," he said, chuckling. "But what do I give you?" He pulled Carla by the waist and sat in the chair next to the window, looking up at her for an answer.

"You can tell me something I don't know!" she said cheerily.

James looked at her curiously, then smiled. "Okay," he said. "A lot of guys think they should be able to have sex with one of every type of girl." He said it with a touch of guilt. "My best friend who came down here with me, for example, has an ongoing list of the different chicks he's fucked, even girlfriends. And I don't think he's ever fucked a black girl before. It's too hard in New York."

Carla was definitely surprised by this forward disclosure from the other side. She had never even thought of it like that before. A list. But Cancun Carla couldn't say it was a bad idea. As a matter of fact, she suddenly wanted to fuck a guy of every race too.

The pair got dressed and James called a cab for her in what to her seemed like typical New York fashion. He then walked her down to the cab and they shared a long-lasting kiss before departing. She looked back at him through the taxi window, thinking how thankful she was for the best sex ever on her final day in Cancun. And for the list idea.

As Carla did her final walk of shame in Zona Hotelero, she entered her shared hotel room to find those bitches Becca and Erica had tossed her luggage out the window and into the pool. Tired and thoroughly fucked, both literally and figuratively, Carla shrugged her shoulders and sighed, calmly rationalizing the act in her head as the result of a drunken escapade. She did an about-face and plopped herself down on one of the squishy hotel couches in the main lobby and went to sleep.

Carla woke to find her hungover peers dragging their luggage to the large buses parked outside. One less thing, she thought to herself, smiling as she humorously pictured her comfy clothes floating in the pool. Her brain turned its attention to the previous night's encounter, and a little jolt coaxed her through the crowd of teens to board one of the buses headed to *el Aeropuerto de Cancun*. She dragged her hands over the tops of the seats as she found the perfect one into which she could sink. She took one last look at the hotel out the window, then leaned back in her seat, smiling at the thought of the newfound slutty self she had discovered among the sparkly sand on the Mexican beaches.

FLIPPING THE SCRIPT

BY MERCEDES CARRERA

He looks blankly at his computer screen. Was he really going through with this? Seven years. Seven years of unwavering support and love. Or at least, what he thought was love. Was it love? Certainly not the love that his father showed his mother, but hell, that was a different place and a different time. Nobody loves with as much duty as an old Southern couple.

That's a digression. After seven *fucking* years, that bitch had the audacity to ask him for a break? Miss Too-Good-For-Herself, Miss Bit-Role as a backup dancer in some nothing music video, thinks she can just walk away for a better deal? Steve might not be Mr. Hollywood, but he's clearing well over an upper class income, with a Los Angeles lifestyle to boot. Successful publishing house, great home in the hills, vacations, and the lifestyle at will.

That fucking cunt.

So it's come to this: staring blankly at AdultFunFriends.com, existential crisis and all. Jesus, this seems like something only desperate men do. It's better than getting too involved though—that eighteen-year-old hot piece of ass who works in purchasing seems to be waving her cunt around a bit too much lately. What a headache this could be.

Here goes. Looking down the list at the Ms. Thirty- to Forty-Five-Somethings, he realizes he's always had a thing for the MILF types. For all his good-boy image in Danville, Tennessee, Steve had certainly fucked his share of the unfulfilled housewives. Not to mention his friend's moms. There was Sheri, mom of David, whose sales executive husband was never home . . . and that bitch loved to screw all over that nicely appointed home, mostly as a "Fuck you" to aforementioned rich husband. There was Donna, mom of Jack (the asshole football jock who beat him out for quarterback), and she loved to get choked and called "Daddy's little whore." That one had issues. There were so many more; hell, part of why Steve left that little town was to get away from horny older housewives who couldn't stand a chance when he got bored.

Secrecy is nothing new to Steve, but this time, it's different. Back then, that was horny teenager stuff; he's a bona fide adult now. Two Masters' degrees, one of them Ivy League, a house in the Hills, a successful business—and *this* was what it's come to? Los Angeles is a notoriously hard place to date, everyone knows that, but by this age, his father had two kids, a mortgage, and three business locations. Yet here Steve is, logging into an infamous website like some fucking john, hoping to get laid by someone in this godforsaken town.

Now, that's a pipe dream if there ever was one.

All right, fuck it. Here goes nothing. Steve sends his photo, credentials, and a sappy-as-shit cover letter (carefully crafted to appeal to every variety of female narcissism) to every decent MILF on the site. It'll probably never come to anything anyway; everyone knows this site is a sausage fest punctuated with whores. But, what the fuck . . . If it doesn't come through, Little Miss Eighteen might get herself the fuck of her life after all.

Not an hour goes by before he gets the first response. Her name is Staci, she's forty-five, divorced, yoga teacher (aren't they all), hot as fuck in the body, seems a little needy. Something, something, new age bullshit, something, something. Somehow, she doesn't seem like someone versed in the particularities of commercial contract code and historical maritime law. Tedious to talk to, but those new age chicks are always sluts, right? But they get attached too . . .

Pass.

Next response is from a face-blurred Asian woman, clearly a hooker. Steve might be a lot of things, but a paying client he is not.

Delete.

Steve starts to think this is a dead end after all, when—

Amy. Twenty-eight, marketing/PR rep, new to California. Looking for a real man, none of this pansy-ass, liberal California bullshit. She likes whiskey, strong men, and a good time. This looks too good to be true. *It's gotta be, but let's pretend it's not. Just send her the throwaway number and see what happens.*

Not long after, the call comes in. 818 area code—the Valley. Who the hell lives in the Valley? Last anyone checked, wasn't the Valley a wasteland of porn stars and decaying aerospace companies?

A timid voice speaks. "Hello?"

"Amy?"

"Um, hi. Um, I think we talked online?"

Suddenly, this is real. *What's the catch? Gotta make sure she knows—I'm no client, just looking for a hot woman to have some fun.* Shake off the Los Angeles end-of-relationship blahs.

Work? Yeah, successful. Nice car. BMW even. Her? Doesn't matter anyway, as long as she's cute enough.

Saturday, seven P.M. Sushi, then maybe back to her place, if all goes well. It's a date.

Versace or Gucci? The shop gal had said the Versace was more elegant, and Gucci more avant-garde. Although, she probably just saw Steve's Tag Heuer and was taking him for a ride. He never could get used to all the bullshit Los Angeles was full of, even ten years later.

Shirt pressed, teeth bleached, car detailed. Amy is cuter in person. Charming, even. Comes from a small town, just another gal trying to make it in this hellhole of lost dreams. Decent family, middle class, state school degree. The kind of gal you'd have married straight out of college if you didn't have bigger dreams and plans.

There's something else though, something vaguely familiar, disarming yet almost docile. She needs a hug but her eyes are begging for something more. Something nasty, kinky. Steve isn't really sure what to make of it—these days if you even look at a woman askance you're setting yourself up for a world of legal hurt, so he puts it out of his mind.

A few Sapporos later and she's asking, almost begging, to take Steve home. She's got an antique record collection, a real fan of Johnny Cash. Kind of cool, in a hipster trying-too-hard kind of way. Steve's been more into EDM himself, but that's only because ex-girlfriend Miss Hollywood Wannabe had a real fetish for the bottle service culture. Never made sense why Los Angeles was so wrapped up in that when all the clubs closed at two A.M. anyway.

OK, here we go. Back to the Valley, which turns out to be NoHo. Okay, decent little loft. She had a roommate, but things got weird and he moved out. She lives alone now.

Good.

She's gonna get some aged whiskey and oh, does he want a chaser?

Whatever she's having is fine.

She's got some interesting furniture for sure. Lots of red, kind of moody. It's nothing like you'd expect. For some reason, she seems like the kind of gal that would have a house full of crap from that pretentious overpriced shabby-chic store in the mall, the one that mass-produces rickety rocking chairs modeled after disintegrating antiques. Instead, there's a lot of leather and velvet, and the concrete walls are painted in some sort of silver glaze. Must have been like this before she moved in.

Strange.

She's got whisky, ginger ale, and water. This is getting too easy, it's almost weird. Most women in this town used their cunt as a bargaining tool unless you were paying upfront, and this gal was acting like they'd done this before. *I should've downloaded that controversial consent app just in case.*

Phil from work knew Steve was on an internet date. *Maybe I should send him my location, just in case. Maybe this chick is a psycho.* Steve was twice her size, but sometimes when he couldn't sleep, he watched those late night shows about women snapping and killing men. It was always the ones you'd least expect.

She'd like to get into something more comfortable. Fine. Kind of 1950s sitcom, but seems like that's kind of her thing, given the old records. It's always something, some sort of pretentious procedure in this town. Nobody just fucks anymore, it's always a show or a play or something. Why the hell did it have to work out that the best commercial law clients are in this desert of vapidity.

Something cracks like a bullwhip. What the fuck was that? He turns around to see her, head to toe, in some bullshit dominatrix getup. Whip, riding crop, ball gag, and a strap-on.

A fucking strap-on with a big black cock.

This fucking cunt. Who the hell does she think she is? Fuck, the men in this town might be a bunch of pussy-ass bitches, but Steve wasn't some weak asshole who wanted to take it up the ass. This was offensive. In fact, downright fucking degrading.

Is it not enough, the degrees, the business, the income, the charming good looks, the Southern charm? Is that what she wants? She wants to see some pussy bend over and take it up the ass? She was in the right town, but not him, and not now. Jesus, this was why Los Angeles women were known for being head cases.

She winds her way over to him, mimicking her best version of drag queen-cum-SS soldier, and he's had quite enough. She flicks her wrist with her riding crop and he almost loses it—grabs her wrist and looks deep into her eyes.

"If you think you're going to play out your twisted b.s. with me, you got another thing coming, sweetheart. Who the fuck do you think you are?"

Aha. She finally realizes she's in over her head.

He isn't some Los Angeles faggot who wants to take it up the ass from a chick in cheap vinyl or anyone else. She says she wants a man, a whisky-drinking, Johnny Cash-listening, real man and this is the shit she pulls?

He's angry.

He's still holding her wrist and he starts backing into her. She's been doing this, working on the side, giving it up the ass to men and making them call her Mistress for $200 an hour. Somewhere along the way, she forgot they don't all like this. She forgot that not every man she meets has a mommy issue and not every asshole she meets online gets his kicks from relinquishing control to a marketing rep from a small town dressed up in pleather.

She's practically panting. "Please don't go. Please."

The disgust he feels is intense enough to be felt as passion by the uninitiated. Something changes. *If this bitch wants to be in control, let's show her what it feels like to be controlled.*

Why is every fucking woman always testing him? Why? It's always something. And when the rubber meets the road, for all the respect he gives and the support of the feminist movement he's outwardly shown (albeit all the while secretly resenting), they all want to be treated like whores.

All of them.

She loves it. He tells her to suck it. *Fucking suck it, you filthy slut.* With relief, she drops to her knees and rips at his pants. He's not even turned on by her, but this woman is going to make up for this little stunt she tried to pull. For the first time, he realizes she, like so many others, really wants to abdicate control. His appeasement of their little whims isn't actually giving them what they want.

He pulls off his belt, obstinately taking his sweet time. This belt is one of the complicated ones, with a counter-intuitive buckle, and he finds her frustration to be mildly amusing. Bit by bit, opening it up, until she's clawing at his zipper and devouring his erect cock.

His cock has always been something of a secret pride of his, and he's certainly never had any complaints. But today, he is even more proud of the girth and strength of his erection. His newfound power is felt in the increasing vigor he is experiencing by realizing he no longer has to be overpowered by women with daddy issues.

She's taking him deep and slowly, and she starts to work faster and harder with her mouth. Messy. Sloppy. She's realizing that her desire all along hasn't been to be anyone's Domme—in reality, she's always wanted to be subordinated, to call a man "Daddy," and be fucked in the face.

Steve grabs her by the back of the head, by the hair, and raises her up to her feet. In a moment of acquiescence, she goes partially limp and, at this moment, they both really know who is in control. And for once, they both know exactly where they're most comfortable—him in charge, and her on her knees.

Not enough. He walks her over, holding the back of her hair, to the hipster couch with the red velvet trim. He's looking deep into her eyes, and their depraved little tango ends when the back of her legs hit the rounded edge of the highly overpriced sofa.

Suddenly, he whips her around, and grabs her by the throat. With a whimper, she whispers "yes" in a last ditch move to pretend that her consent still actually means a damn thing. His face is against the back of her head, and she's locked into place by his strong grip. Steve reaches down and unzips the dominatrix getup she put herself in. Fortunately, it zips right open and slips off, to where her previously bound legs are now naked in the middle, exposing her dripping wet pussy.

What a gorgeous vagina, he thinks, as he realizes she's as wet as he is hard. Her body is aching to feel that hard cock in her, and Steve is now realizing that part of the power is to not give them everything they want of him. He teases her slowly, running the head of his cock over her moist cunt, up and down, and up between the split in her tight young ass. He slaps his penis over her—*slap slap slap*—and each time he does, Amy writhes in anticipation, just hoping, begging, pleading silently in her head that he'll stick it right in.

Finally, he concedes and pushes his cock through the tight pink opening of her pussy. She tightens her grip around his cock but also, in a contradictory fashion, accepts every inch of him. His hands are still on her throat and now his other arm is around her waist, both holding her up and bracing her against the rolled arm of the couch. Her legs are open wide, braced by the stiletto points of the vinyl boots she got on sale at the local stripper shop.

He's fucking her faster and faster now, and her legs are shaking and quivering. He smiles. It's so much, it's too much, the feeling of being completely taken is what she's always needed and craved. Her legs give way and she lets out a screaming orgasm—relief and ecstasy in what he recognizes as the feeling of being taken, being dominated, and for once not having to be the one in control.

Steve feels her cum all over his cock and it brings him right to the edge. *Not yet*, he thinks. *No fucking way am I done with this experience, and it's almost too much.* He pulls out, and turns her around, still holding her firmly against his body.

He looks deep into her eyes, and sees his own passion reflected in her. Finally, he can be the strong one, no more of this hidden resentment, and finally she can submit without testing every man who crosses her path.

She goes to kiss him, and he puts his hand across her mouth. The whimper with which she responds indicates acquiescence. He walks her backwards to the body of the ornamented velvet sofa and lays her down. Coming close to her, still with his hand over her mouth, Steve's gaze comes inches away from Amy's. They'd be sharing the same breath if his hand weren't in the way.

He thrusts his still throbbing cock deep into her willing pussy and fucks her with even more passion now, looking deeply into her eyes with each movement. He is going deeper, longer, faster, until she can't take it, her body writhing beneath him, quivering, shaking, until it seems as though she's lost all control.

He can't take it any longer either. It's time now. He knows he shouldn't but fuck it, it's time to do something he'd usually not do, which is in keeping with everything else this evening. He shakes, and the power of his orgasm surges through him as he releases his hot, full load deep into her still-quivering cunt. She yelps, knowing she's being filled with his hot creamy cum, and just at that moment, he releases his hand and finally kisses her, looking deeply into her eyes.

They both know now exactly why they've felt so unfulfilled, and they both know now exactly who and what they really are meant to be.

Please let this happen again, Steve thinks. And as he looks in her eyes, he sees she feels it too.

HUSBAND AND WIFE

BY NINA HARTLEY

The Husband made his living as a writer, director, magazine editor, and author.

The Wife made her living in front of the camera.

They were Dom/Sub-oriented, and loved entertaining other power-exchange loving women. Their dungeon had been seen in many videos, but the most fun happened off-camera, after hours, when The Couple could fully explore each of the letters in BDSM, in any way they chose. Husband was dominant, Wife a bisexual, top-heavy switch; their playmates had two experienced people working on them simultaneously. He loved having another him to help show their guests a good time, and She was equally thrilled to put on her riding boots and butch it up. Always clear about what they offered, one would be surprised—or perhaps not—at how many women thought that an evening spent as their "love slave," followed by a home-cooked meal, sounded like a simply splendid time.

Husband and Wife particularly appreciated service-oriented, sexually masochistic women, much like Wife, allowing them all to explore the event horizon between pain and pleasure.

They'd done it so often over their sixteen years together they had the whole experience down to a science. First, everyone was tested at the clinic the professionals used in order to play Porno-Style: condom-free, coupled with external ejaculation. On the morning of the appointed day, Husband and Wife spent some time planning out the future for their guest, taking into account a) what she liked, and b) what they liked.

During many years together, they'd mastered the art of the pre-date negotiation, making the actual date feel effortlessly smooth, like Fred and Ginger taking a turn around the dance floor. They then set up the dungeon space according to the agreed-upon parameters before eating a nice lunch. Afterwards, they pulled toys, gear, cuffs, wardrobe, collars, butt plugs, whips, floggers, canes, and of course, some good smut with which to transition out of the normal pace of the day and into the Dream Time of BDSM.

The Couple preferred minimal, yet evocative costuming to set the mood. Wife was usually in a leather collar, leather body harness, and tall boots. Husband donned high, shiny riding boots (the better for kissing), and a leather military-style envelope hat (aka a "cunt cap"). The guest arrived at five P.M. sharp to play before dinner, as one rarely felt sexy on a full stomach. Besides, eating after playing gave one so much more to talk about, especially when everyone remained naked.

Tall Girl recently visited the Couple on an afternoon. She stood five-foot-ten, with strong, long legs, a pretty shaved vulva complete with a perfectly meaty clit, small firm breasts, silky dark hair, and a sparkling smile. Due to her height, she was permitted to remain barefoot, instead of wearing the six-inch fetish pumps the Couple put on their more petite guests. She arrived right on time, as was her way. The Couple's first move was to strip her naked before kissing her hello. Once the pleasantries were over, Tall Girl put on her collar and cuffs, which had been laid out on the table, while the Couple took turns distracting her by fondling and stroking her tender bits. Because of her athletic build, their favorite costume for her was a ribbed white tank strategically cut off just above the legal limit. It was very hard to be modest in such an outfit. Her fresh, dark maroon pedicure was well suited to her brunette good looks. Enforcing the house motto of "Everything is permitted except modesty," Tall Girl sat between Them, one of her legs draped over one of each of theirs, conveniently displaying her assets. The Couple perused a pile of hard-core illustrations from the folder marked "Faves." It amused them to see which images made Tall Girl squeal, sigh, laugh, point, or wiggle, one or the other maintaining a hand on her pussy at all times, idly keeping her engine revving for later.

People who enjoy impact play usually prefer either a "thumpy" or a stinging sensation, though some are quite happy with either. "Thumpsters" like to feel the impact deeply in the muscles, while sting-lovers crave the sharpness of a surface hit. Tall Girl loved a good thumping, allowing the Couple to use their heaviest implements on her. They took turns employing their fists to hit her pectorals above her perky boobs, her stomach, her ass, and her thighs. Wife particularly enjoyed the blissful look on Tall Girl's face when she was hit with thumpy things. Of course she endured stinging things too, knowing Husband loved them, and the reward for enduring them was more fucking. But with her, the thump was where it was at.

Wife found it very liberating to hit someone really hard in just the right place, only to see their face get all dreamy while hearing them giggle and sigh. Tall Girl had six inches on Wife, allowing Wife to use almost all of her might; while Husband, on the other hand, needed to pull it back a bit. Still, Tall Girl loved to be between them, being punched by both at the same time. Wife loved working out on her, finding the activity much more fun than going to the gym. By the time the thumping was over, everyone was breathing heavily and grinning in anticipation.

After the warm-up in the living room, the Couple clipped Tall Girl's hands behind her using a carabineer and walked her back to the play space. The room spread out before them: the cage, the shiny black rubber floor, the bondage bed, electric vacuum pump, suspension bar, spanking horse, and, of course, the thickly padded bounce wall with the fucking stool already placed in front of it. Lube and baby wipes were set out wherever they might be needed, as well as Magic Wand vibrators, all plugged in with the business ends covered in fresh condoms. Every detail had been attended to, the better to pull off a flawless experience.

As was their way with Tall Girl, she first was splayed on the dungeon bed with her hands clipped above her head to some loose chains, limiting the use of her arms. Wife lay on top of her, kissing her hungry mouth and grinding her thigh into Tall Girl's pussy, while Husband lay beside them, soaking up the vision of her relative helplessness. Wife put on sexy black latex gloves ("Sanitary is a state of fact while dirty is a state of mind," she always said), lubed up Tall Girl's smooth outer parts, before handing her the control valve for the suction machine. Placing a long, clear tube with a three-inch diameter opening just so on her vulva, Wife flipped on the motor and had Tall Girl occlude the valve. This immediately sucked her moist, pink flesh into the tube.

"Up or down?" Wife asked, to check on proper placement. It took only one or two minor adjustments to find the perfect spot. It was easy to tell when it happened, as Tall Girl let out a little yelp of pleasure and surprise. Then it was up to her to torture herself as hard and as long as she wanted. Tall Girl, like most of The Couple's play partners, was always meaner to herself then they'd be to her, but they were her parts, so she'd know. Said parts slid up the walls of the tube a good three inches, puffing up obscenely and making them more tender for afterwards, while the motor whirred tirelessly away.

While Tall Girl essentially sucked her own pussy, Wife lubed up the outside of her thigh so Husband could use Tall Girl as a masturbatory object while enjoying her efforts. After ten minutes, Wife popped the tube off and Husband got on, having been ready to fuck her for a while by then. Tall Girl made lovely sounds when he entered her eager pussy and her pretty bare feet were exposed in mid-air above his shoulders. Only one thing for it: foot caning! Husband loved to see the emotion in the faces of the women while Wife hurt their feet. He could feel their insides clutch his hardness with every stroke of the cane. Masochistic women seem to find the sensation particularly intense due to the concentration of nerve endings in such a small area. Foot caning had a long and honorable tradition in BDSM sex play, and an even longer (if not so pleasant) history as a punishment.

It even had a name: bastinado.

Wife held one foot in her hand and asked Husband if he was ready for her to cane Tall Girl. When he said he was, she caned Tall Girl's left foot five times, stopping only when there was a specific tone to the yelp emitted. Tall Girl complained that Wife was mean, to which she replied that it was only in the service of pleasing Sir. Tall Girl accused Wife of lying, which was a bad move, as Wife now had Tall Girl's right foot in her hand. Five more strokes of the cane ended with a pitiful yelp when Wife was mean-for-real, but not too much so. In their world, a masochist calling a dominant "mean" is a compliment. Besides, it only took a few more thrusts from Husband before Tall Girl was asking permission to cum. He gave it, of course, not being the kind of dominant stupid enough to deny orgasms to his partners.

After that first fuck, Husband used his fingers in Tall Girl's pussy (they liked to go back and forth between fingers, dick, and toys as penetrating objects,) while Wife donned a fresh pair of latex gloves and started warming up Tall Girl's butt. Tall Girl was not averse to butt play, but because she didn't get much of it, hers felt like a virgin butt once again. No worries. All butts needed to be coaxed and seduced each time, no matter how often they saw action. Husband lay on his side and used his right hand in her pussy as Wife rolled onto her stomach and used her left hand in Tall Girl's butt. It didn't take long for her to relax enough to allow two fingers in easily.

That was when Husband and Wife started a dance between their fingers, easy to do through the thin membrane of Tall Girl's perineum. Tall Girl said it felt like she was being double-penetrated without any of the awkward body mechanics. Next, Wife slipped in a small stainless steel plug, blotted any excess lube, and she was good to go, tidy on the outside while being stuffed on the inside. Butt plugs were great for sex as they made the dick feel different in the pussy and the pussy feel different to the dick. It was like all the fun of swapping partners, without all the drama.

The rest of the date was devoted to fucking Tall Girl doggie-style, missionary, in the bar stool set to hip level, pushed up against the bounce wall (all the fun of fucking in a sling with none of the hassle of setting one up). Wife wore her favorite strap-on harness and used Tall Girl's favorite dildo. Husband and Wife did a mini-gangbang, each of them fucking Tall Girl on each piece of equipment.

But then, something interesting happened after Husband whipped Tall Girl (strung up on the suspension bar on tiptoe) to tears: he got a hankering to fuck and hurt Wife, too, instantly changing the double-Dom/single-sub action to a solo-Dom/sister-sub scene. Tall Girl jumped up and down with glee; she was so eager to see Husband hurt Wife.

Husband got his favorite cane and Wife sat down on the

dungeon bed. Knowing what was coming next, she held up her tits as he caned the tops, laying down four or five bright red stripes before hitting his final target: her nipples. That always made Wife yelp in the frequency that said, "That's it!" Meaning, just the right combination of genuine, that's-enough pain, and sexy adrenaline rush (Wife knew hurting willing partners turned Husband on). Just for good measure, he caned her ass, too, which she always loved. He then had their guest put her tail in the air while Wife put her pussy in Tall Girl's face and watched in the mirror the lovely line from the Wife to Tall Girl, to him, all fucking and sucking in perfect syncopation. Tall Girl, outside of playing with the Couple, was a dedicated lesbian and an advanced oral expert, to put it mildly. It was amazing for Wife to feel Husband's energy come through Tall Girl's mouth, being fucked by proxy. Tall Girl was ecstatic, being penetrated while having her face buried in the promised land of pussy.

After the train action on the bed, Husband had the women nose-to-tail over the sides of the spanking horse. That way, Tall Girl could get an up close view of him fucking Wife, and Wife could do the same when he came around to the other side. He fucked Tall Girl and then had Wife suck Tall Girl off of him before fucking Wife and then doing the same to Tall Girl. He also had each of the women suck her own juices off of him before plunging into the next. They couldn't decide which was hotter, tasting the other, or tasting herself.

Since porno rules dictate external ejaculation, there eventually came the time when the guest was put on the floor, and her mouth was put to good purpose. Tall Girl blew Husband while Wife used her favorite dildo and a Magic Wand on herself, surfing the energy so Husband and Wife came at the same time. Husband gave Tall Girl a load on her tits.

Whew! What a blast! Tall Girl took off the Couple's boots,

and they all relaxed on the bed in a happy heap before Wife got up to make dinner, leaving Husband and guest to clean up.

The guest of honor was fed, showered, dressed, and on her way by eleven that night, and the Couple was ensconced on the couch watching the news, a happy smile playing about their lips. All in all, it had been six very well-spent hours.

MID-TWENTY-TEENS

BY DANA DEARMOND

It's a hot August night, but there's a breeze; it's the third year of the California drought.

I've been single for about a year. Free food and awkward conversation is pretty much all dating in LA has to offer, and I'm starving for more. More regularly than not, I lurk Instagram for beautiful, shirtless, self-absorbed model-types. Sometimes I just look, and sometimes I leave them a heart-eyes emoji in the comments section of a bathroom mirror selfie. I don't really expect any attention in return, it just feels nice to objectify an attractive young man—it's my mid-twenty-teens! Aka: being a single creative in my thirties, residing in the downtown of a major metropolitan US city alone with my two hairless cats. Don't worry, it doesn't carry the stigma of "lonely cat lady" that it would have a decade ago. Think of me more as Michelle Pfief-fer's Catwoman in the Tim Burton 1992 Batman, right after her boss tried to kill her (spoiler alert).

At any rate, the weather is right, and tonight I go out to stalk my prey.

Wearing high-waisted jeans and a flannel shirt from J. Crew, I try to blend in meekly. I'm comfortable enough with my androgynous femininity to pull off this look I like to call the "Lumber Jill." Unlike the other girls who show up to this 1980s-themed club on a Thursday night, I fucking remember the eighties. I was there.

The children of the nineties bop along with the music they might have heard in passing as a suggestion on their Pandora Prince station. They try on the costume of the era: American Apparel disco pants paired with off-the-shoulder tops, complete with jelly bracelets or a single plastic statement earring procured from Etsy. In the crowd I see someone I recognize: an Instagram boy. We've direct messaged back and forth before, and he looks different with his shirt on but I am still pleased with his face. I move toward him.

His name is Billy. And he is *such* a Billy. Effortlessly messy curls in his hair, a devilish smile and the flippant air of not really giving a shit that was ushered in by the millennial generation. His body is nearly perfect; probably because at his age he's still producing human growth hormone The definition in his biceps peeks out from the sleeves of his bootleg eighties band tour T-shirt. I'm picturing the rippling six-pack abs under this threadbare "vintage" shirt he lies about getting as a hand-me-down from his dad, when I notice he's not alone.

I approach the boys, sandy-haired, surfer-type Billy complemented perfectly by his cliché tall-dark-handsome friend—a Jared, apparently—who has an olive complexion and is well-dressed in a suit. I learn the childhood bestie is just visiting from New York which is perfect for me, because this guarantees that if I bang him, I will not run into him at my favorite local dives and get repeatedly cock-blocked by him. As a . . . let's say, *sexually empowered and uninhibited woman,* getting cock-blocked by past fucks has been a huge problem for me. Los Angeles is a much smaller town than one might think.

Introductions are not necessary because Billy recognizes me from the internet, too. Cheekily, I express my excitement that he's brought along a friend and ask if they are going to kiss later. They laugh. I laugh. We are breaking the ice. Drinks are consumed. The boys take turns flirting with me while the other's back is turned. They compete for my attention, and I am living for it. As Billy talks to a girl he knows from one of his DJing gigs in West Hollywood, Jared caresses my ass through the pocket of my dark denim mom-jeans. He close-talks in my ear, some bullshit about his life on the Upper West Side, which I utterly do not give one shit about. I just hope his friend will see the way he's touching me, fall into a fit of jealousy, inciting the boys to fight over me.

Another round of drinks, and now it's pretty boy Billy's turn flirting. He's a little rough around the edges; I want to mommy him, I want to fold his laundry. But mostly, I want him to fuck me really hard in his parents' house where I assume he lives. I deduce from the fact he lives in this town that he's probably completely emotionally unavailable and good for approximately three bangs. Three bangs, that's the limit—five if I really, really like their dick. After five, I ghost on a guy completely, block their number and all social media. If I were a man and did this sort of thing to ladies, I would definitely be branded a total asshole and misogynist. Good thing I have a pussy.

Now it's just a matter of choosing. Both guys have a lot of pros going for them, including being on the dumb side and most likely having very young girlfriends. Although I wouldn't fuck a married man, I have no issue fucking somebody else's boyfriend.

Billy perkily suggests, "Let's go to your house!"

Oh, I don't think so. I'm not letting these heathens into my house. There is no way I'm letting either of them know where I live. My home is private, off-limits to fuck boys like these. There is a hotel literally upstairs but we have drunk past the point of negotiating something as logical as checking into a room. Besides,

I'm not completely certain either of these jokers would be able to afford a night's stay at this upscale boutique hotel in Korea Town.

They call an Uber and I get in without knowing which direction it might take us. Growing up, I was taught never to talk to strangers, never to get into a car if you don't know the person driving, and especially don't go anywhere with boys if you're unchaperoned. But the invention of Uber has lulled me into a strange comfortability with getting into any car with a stranger, and it's pretty clear by now that tonight is the night I set out to break all conventions. Besides, statistically I am far more likely to be killed by a family friend, family member, or boyfriend/spouse (of which I have neither). I repeat this fact to myself intermittently so I don't get cold feet and not at least make out and dry hump one of these dudes. Squirming in my seat with anticipation, my phone battery at less than 20 percent, I know I am all in for whatever transpires. Even if I get murdered by these adorable dickheads.

The car arrives at a house at the top of the Hollywood Hills—so Billy's daddy is rich! I enter the house and am immediately intoxicated by the aroma of filthy young men. Dirty laundry on the bathroom floor, unopened mail scattered around indiscriminately, tubs of protein powder in the kitchen, along with an expansive collection of empty liquor bottles in a row atop the cabinets as trophies of previous wild nights. A stoneware plate with white powder cut up into lines is just sitting there out in the open. Mom and Dad definitely don't live here; I am inside a hot-rich-boy squatter house. Aka, heaven.

I have yet to find a term that describes men as *coquettish*, because the word in and of itself is in reference to a flirtatious female, often younger, looking to win male affection. But these boys were being just that: Coquettish.

There's something about millennials that is so relaxed about sex that I find both shocking and adorable. It is clear that I don't have to choose one or the other; this is their "thing." I ask coyly if they've ever done something like this before, hoping that they'll say no, and I am about to be the one to finally turn them out. I'm going to seal the deal. That joke about them kissing? That was exactly the seed they needed to be planted to nurture their curiosity.

But to my disappointment, Billy chirps, "We've done this, together, what? Three times?" This dance has been rehearsed; they fancy themselves gigolos. And that's just fine with me, I suppose.

We are all on the same page. No baited traps necessary. The hot summer night air is hanging heavy and it wants me to be naked and touched and have my sweat lapped from my body. They take turns, at first, like a couple of tomcats batting around a mouse before ripping into it. They caress and kiss me, and I hardly notice they are slowly disrobing me. Billy scurries off to the bedroom and Jared, now shirtless, hoists me over his shoulder like a caveman, following Billy and throwing me down onto the bed. I can see the bulges of their super-hard cocks through their pants. I stroke them both, as my floral print cotton thong becomes soaked with pussy juice.

One kisses me deeply while the other teases my hole through my panties, as if occupying one end will distract me from the other. I feel everything, my body becomes electric. I hear a condom packet opening, then a condom rolling down the shaft of Billy's cock as his buddy continues tonguing my mouth hungrily. His cock pushes into me and I think about how seldom I ever have sex using a condom. I've been having unprotected sex for over a decade in the adult film industry and I love the feeling of a rock-hard dick inside me, but there's something extra kinky and even maybe taboo about using a condom at this point in my life. A condom is a permission slip to be a filthy whore.

I get fucked in just about every possible devil's three-way position. Doggie-style with dick in mouth, missionary while getting face-fucked on the edge of the bed, reverse cowgirl while snorting a line of ketamine off a dick, double blowjob. I make the cocks touch in my mouth, a thin layer of my sloppy throat slime is the only thing between the boys. When they fuck me, I feel them gravitate towards each other. I fantasize that they want to be with each other so badly that they rip me in half and finally give in to their deepest homoerotic instincts on top of my discarded body parts.

I look up at their heaving bodies, their abs rippling. They are panting as I stroke them. Their foreheads touch, their sweat combines before dripping down on my writhing naked body and into my mouth. I am envisioning them just one inch closer and their lips meeting. I am tasting the salty sweat and dreaming of it finally happening for them.

Billy shoots a load; the salty and sweet combination of sweat and cum fills my mouth. A few seconds later Jared cums too, probably from seeing Billy glaze me with jizz. I rush off to the bathroom to take a whore's bath in the sink and image them alone. They probably didn't kiss. But I like to imagine they did. Not for me—for each other.

There is just enough power in my phone to call an Uber and whisk myself home.

I leave, block their numbers and all social media, and ghost completely so I can remember them just as I left.

Perfect, alone, together . . . probably kissing.

IN, OUT

BY YHIVI

The greatest gifts I've received have been the toughest to name. There's a depth to them that words just can't touch. That's not to say this existential challenge has dissuaded me from trying to find the words—to understand and communicate what it is that makes those gifts so special. In fact, when I receive something I register as special, it inspires the inclination to push past that surface feeling—to commemorate the moment, to document it.

Most of my day-to-day is a matter of that very push. Or pull, depending on how you look at it. Every interaction, however minute or massive has the potential of breaking down some wall. Walls that I've put up myself. Walls that you've put up yourself. Walls that are merely a figment.

They've been put there to protect the body, the mind, the heart.

A constant cycle of barriers.

For a larger part of my life, I've lived by that cycle. With brief interruptions of unapologetic ignorance to the dangers of an open heart. But when you put up a wall, your barricade doesn't just keep negative consequence out. It also locks you in complacency.

I now work every day to break them down. Discovered strength in this vulnerability, and warmth in the willingness to subject myself to the cold possibility of rejection. In pain and discomfort, I've found the most growth and relief: a release from the theory that the best thing to do for yourself is hide your light from others. I shine brighter now than when I lived by fear, and every risk has lit the way to a life more vibrant than safety could ever conceive.

Among the wreckage of walls long since torn down, I've fashioned a haven for my heart, still healing, still detaching from an existence very present in the hearts of many others. I fill this refuge with trinkets of love and hope I find living in every honest interaction or blessed experience.

Our interaction provides a solace and inspiration to nurture the parts of myself I hold dearest to me. I hope I do the same for you.

Your companionship gives way to a remarkable flow and exchange of gifts that words could never adequately describe.

In, out. In, out. In, out.

Your touch enlivens a sanctuary of light within me. With each caress, with every stroke, it glows brighter.

There's a balance in our exchange. A back and forth.

A push, and pull.

It's equally humbling and elevating, the way we embrace our contradictions to celebrate each other. I feel your strength, yet you hold me with a tenderness I can only describe as the softest presence I've ever experienced.

Our moments together are beyond words. Your eyes tell stories to which your mouth just couldn't do justice. Likewise, my embrace says things that only your bare skin could understand.

In, out. In, out. In, out.

You can feel it in the spaces between your fingers, running along the lines of your body. At times you don't notice, at others, you feel like it's the only thing you have left to hold onto. But you can't hold it—not for long. So it ebbs, and it flows.

I want to fill any space that's left between you and me. Listen to it crash between your lips as you let go. I want to take it from you.

In, out. In, out. In, out.

Slowly, you seem to feel it more as I touch your body, and as you touch mine. It's becoming heavier and heavier with each moment. Heavy upon our lips, as they shift to get closer to one another. Heavy upon our eyelids. Heavy upon the nape of our necks, and in between the cracks that sit between our skin and the fabric of our clothes.

The pattern of your breath emanates along the curve of my ears as we pull each other closer, and now it's anything but heavy. You seem to get lighter with every movement.

In, out. In, out. In, out.

I feel like I'm floating away, but I can't recall the last time I was ever so present. We drift higher, higher, higher. We're filling the spaces in between our bodies and the rest of the room with a melody that aches to be sung, over, and over. We continue to fill one another up.

Pushing your lips against mine, my mouth opens—in, out. In, out. In, out. Our moans blend with each other's before they touch the air around us. And suddenly, those spaces don't feel like a separation anymore—not when every inch of them carries this bottomless fervor we're exchanging more fiercely with each gliding moment.

I feel us expanding, every second more expansive than the last. I want to saturate myself in each instant more than the one before, but I am simultaneously pushing for the next. Going back and forth between each fraction of each second with the urge to stay right there forever, and push to experience as much of you as I can hold.

In, out. In, out. In, out.

The word "tremble" suggests a tone of unsureness, or a lack of intention. But as we do just that—tremble. Each shudder speaks to a confidence that encompasses my whole body, an intention I embrace with an intensity matched only by the one I can feel pulsing inside of you too.

Every part of me is captivated by every part you've been so brave to share. Both tangible and not, the beauty you hold within yourself holds me in adoration.

There is no fragment of my truest self that isn't exploding.

In, out. In, out. In, in, in.

In.

It's heavy again, and the thumping inside our chests brings us deeper into each other. Around, above, below, against.

The air between us has been shifting with a solemn fluidity—a eulogy borne by its own subject.

THE RENTAL CAR GUY

BY CHARLOTTE CROSS

There you were, staring at a computer screen with one of your employees as I barged through the door.

"We have a problem," I barked at the lady behind the counter. The annoyance in my voice I'm sure was more than apparent, but I was right—we had problems.

My problem was that I hated being back home in the Middle of Nowhere, West Virginia. My problem was that I was stuck at my conservative parents' house where there was no privacy, and therefore I wasn't able to have the three-hours' worth of bed-shaking sex every night like I needed.

And your problem? Well, honey, your problem was me.

I came into the Renter-Prize Center that day because I'm a horrible driver. Let's say I've been awarded more speeding tickets and totaled more cars than your average twenty-one-year-old brat. Reckless, carefree driving had always been my problem—little did I know that today, it would become my solution.

I made my way over to the counter, where you greeted me with a warm smile. Extending your arm out to shake my hand, you beamed. "Hello, welcome to Renter-prize. I'm the guy that's here to solve all of your problems."

Or at least, that's how I heard it.

Hello, handsome. I'm horny and you're not from around here.

If you were from around here, we would have known each other. We would have gone to the same schools, youth group, and secret high school parties. You would have been a football player that I cheered for under the Friday night lights. You would have been best friends with my high school sweetheart, meaning I would have been best friends with yours. Our Saturday nights would have been reserved for double dates and your family would have attended the little Southern Baptist Church that my father preached at every Sunday morning. But most importantly, I would've already fucked you in the naughtiest way possible.

You would have already been one of my dirty little secrets.

I was a cheerleader, class president, preacher's daughter, and the slut. My daddy thought I was saving myself for marriage. That day was supposed to be my special day, the day I finally wed the man that he and God planned to give me to. Little did he know, I wore my purity ring as I proudly sucked off half the county, all before the end of my senior year. Sorry, Daddy, you missed out on the deflowering of the bride. The funny thing is, nobody ever talked about any my wrongdoings. They were too scared of my parents—because who would want to be the one that tells the preacher his baby girl was nothing more than a loose whore? Certainly not you. My dad might have been hell-bent on saving those eighteen-year-old boys from their ungodly desires, but nothing he did could ever save them from me. I was hell in a Sunday school dress. I never missed my chance with a boy.

So, that was how I know we didn't know each other.

In the South, we call someone like you a tall drink of water. You towered over me as I scanned your strongly sculpted body. Your presence was almost as strong as my desire to be fucked like a porn star on her first day of auditions. Not only tall, but you were tan with broad shoulders. If you were to flex, your arms would have busted the seams of your nicely tailored suit. Most girls would have been intimidated; but not me, I've seen your type before.

Boys like you are the boys I live to destroy.

Where I come from, you're everything a girl's mama would pray for her baby to find: a charming guy, easy on the eyes, with a steady job and a firm handshake. The kind of man that makes all the sweet, southern girls' hearts flutter. You might have been the man of their dreams, where I come from. But to me, you were nothing more than the boy I'd use to fulfill my fantasies. My heart was set on devouring you.

And I almost always got what I want.

"Are you renting a car from us today?" you asked with a sunny, bright smile.

"No, not exactly. Well, kind of, I guess . . . " I couldn't help stuttering my words as I got lost in your gaze. "I'm renting a car from The Renter-Prize Center inside of Charlotte-Douglas Airport since it's the closest airport to home that will let someone under the age of twenty-five rent a car."

In West Virginia, you have to be fourteen to marry your cousin, but don't even think about renting a car until you're nearly thirty. And we wonder why there are so many jokes about how backwards West Virginians are.

"Honey, let me tell you about how unlucky I was last night on my way into town!" I attempted to find that Southern charm that I only brought out every now and then, when I was adamant on getting my way. Those Los Angeles boys could never resist it; I prayed it would have the same effect on you.

"I was drivin' down the four lane, headed to my mama's and daddy's house real late last night. And as I's comin' past Mr. Bowles' Auto Shop, the one up there on the right, just before the broken stop light—you know the one I'm talkin' about! Well, honey, as soon as I hit the bottom of the hill, I felt that little Chevy run clean over some type of road kill. But honestly, dear, I didn't think nothin' of it! I just kept on and then that little light on the dash came on!"

You hung on to my every word as the intelligent, well-spoken voice inside of my head rolled her bratty eyes at me. *Listen, brainiac, we don't have time for good decisions!* I silently scolded her. *The devil inside of us is horny and will get some spontaneous stranger-cock in this dripping wet pussy that we share whether you like it or not!* She had no choice but to oblige my deviant desires. After all, she's the one that had to coexist with the sex devil inside me. And that devil sure was a force to be reckoned with.

"Ah, yes! Did you call earlier this morning? My deepest apologies, ma'am! Let me see what I can do to make this trip back home more pleasant for you!" Your smile was a breath of fresh air; I was having trouble not getting lost in it.

You continued on about everything you were going to do to fix my problem, but I was struggling to focus on anything but the thought of seeing you stripped down to nothing.

"I don't have anything I can switch you out in today, but why don't you take a seat in my office. I'll make some calls about getting a new tire on your current rental. It shouldn't take too long." Chills went up my spine as you gently placed your left hand on my back and guided me into your office.

When you're as sexually charged as me, it doesn't take much to create a sticky wet spot in the cotton lining of your silky Victoria Secret panties. I'd grown accustomed to carrying an extra pair of sexy slut-panties around in my purse for this exact reason. It was almost unfair, how much my pussy dripped with desire, but I was sure you wouldn't complain. Your office was quite plain; I wasn't the least bit impressed by it. The air-conditioning unit was on full blast, making me regret that I stopped wearing bras when I left my old life behind. The nipples attached to my natural 32C-cup breasts stood at full attention—they may as well have been two new Army recruits headed off to boot camp.

The only things that your office possessed were two chairs, a cheap-looking wooden desk, a bobblehead of Muhammad Ali, and my sexual demons that slowly infected every enclosed area I entered. You left me waiting; patiently and quiet.

That was where you sealed your fate.

Hadn't your mama ever told you that idle hands do the devil's work? Maybe you'd never heard that Southern saying before, since you weren't from here. Never let a good-girl-gone-rogue sit alone to think. Thinking leads to plotting, and plotting leads to destruction—and do you know what I was planning on destroying this time?

You.

I could already picture it: I'm straddling your desk, wearing nothing but ruby red lingerie. The lace is trailing down my young, tight body, accentuating everything you loved about a woman. My firm natural breasts are pushed up, begging you to run your fingers around the top of my C-cups. Every last bit of my body is tan except for the areas usually covered by my tiny string bikini when I go down to Venice Beach on my days off. My body is highlighted in all the right places, showing you the parts that can't be exposed to the general public. My garter belt and stockings drive you insane. I can see that you want nothing more than to run your tongue from the tip of my left nipple, across my belly button, finishing at the end of my throbbing clit. I open my legs slowly, inviting you in with my favorite sultry look. My voice is at a low, sexy whisper, begging you to come closer to me, begging you to enter me. You move towards me with your fully erect cock. Pushing me on my back, you part my legs at the knees and prepare to dive in. You are Moses and my legs are the Red Sea;

their only job is to guide you on your journey to the Promised Land. Using your mouth, you make your way up my body with gentle kisses. The only thing I see are two eyes that remind me of our old barn door, flecks of mahogany infected with speckles of black sin. Those daring eyes lock with mine as you bury your head deep between my thighs. I start gyrating my hips up and down as you continue to tease me with your experienced tongue. I'd do anything if you were to take me right here in this office, pinning me to the top of your desk. I'm begging for you to fill me with the gift you have hanging between your legs, but you won't give in to my desires. You love teasing me because I'm pretending to be helpless, lying underneath you right now. You grab the base of your cock and thrust it deep inside me. My eyes roll back in my head as I gasp with surprise. The first penetration is the best. The way you pump your cock in and out of me sends electricity to the tips of my freshly pedicured toes. It feels like I'm shuffling my feet across the carpet of my bedroom back in the city. This sex is electric. You're stimulating every nerve ending in my body. You force your sex in and out of my tight hole, making my body convulse.

Really though, I was just grinding my pussy against the chair in your office. I was making a mess in your chair, but I didn't care. Too busy envisioning you doing dirty things to me, I didn't care about any mess I could potentially make. My sex demons loved these daydreams. They were running through me, unable to contain their excitement. They were working me up for an intense orgasm, when—

"Here you go! It's all fixed up for you, Miss."

As you re-entered your office, my heart turned cold, and I almost jumped through the roof trying to hide the evidence of my masturbation. I remembered that my nipples were as hard as the diamond ring that should have been on my left hand by now. And I had created a damp spot on your cloth-covered chair. Snapping back into reality, I cleared my throat and composed myself. We stared at each other for a little longer than most people would find comfortable.

"Th-thank you so much!" I stuttered. "I really appreciate how attentive you were to my needs today." Then, I broke away from your beautiful, needle-like eyes.

"You're more than welcome, and here's a business card just in case you need anything else while you're in town. Please . . . don't hesitate to call me."

Anyone could feel the way you were fucking me with your mysteriously dark mind and boy, was I fucking you back. We stood there for what felt like an eternity; our breathing in sync, as if we were waltzing—only, we weren't. We were completely stuck and dancing was the last thing on my mind. I imagined what we should have already done by now. I should've grabbed you by the face, kissing you with undeniable passion. You should've lifted me up as I wrapped my legs around your strong body, pushing me up against the wall, kissing me back. Your hands should have been getting lost in my hair, tearing me to pieces. You should have stripped me down to nothing, exposing every last vulnerable part of my body.

You should've been fucking me.

But none of this was happening. You were too busy escorting me out the door, sending me and all of my evil back out into the real, non-waltzing world.

How unfair.